Edited by

Francesco Verso

Arabilious

Anthology of Arab Futurism

Edited by Cristina Jurado and Francesco Verso

Copyediting by Sally McCorry

Published by Associazione Future Fiction
Via Valentiniano 40 – 00145 Roma
TAX ID. 97962020588

Copyright © 2024 Future Fiction

The story "A Jaha in the Metaverse" by Fadi Zaghmout has been translated from Arab into English by Rana Asfour.
The story "Cinammon Flavor Gum" by Maria Dadouch and have been translated from Arab into English by Simone Noto.
The story appared for the first time on the "Markaz Review": https://the-markaz.org/a-jaha-in-the-metaverse-fiction-by-fadi-zaghmout/
The introduction to Arabilious has been translated from Italian to English by Sally McCorry.

Designed and typeset by Alda Teodorani.

Cover illustration by Eugenia Ponzo.

Title: *Arabilious—Anthology of Arab Futurism*
© 2024 Future Fiction, Roma
I edition July 2024
ISBN: 9788832077988
info@futurefiction.org

ARABILIOUS: AN INTRODUCTION

Historically, narration is a fundamental part of the Arab tradition, however we now need to ask where it has gone. [...] First of all, innovation passes through imagination. Science Fiction is a wonderful bridge that can unite these two things: imagination and innovation.
Yasmine Khan

It might be neither right nor appropriate to consider as "science fiction" the narrative of authors from Arabic countries looking to the future and exploring the influence of technology and scientific progress on society. The term, coined in the West, might not represent the complexity of the thoughts and cultural wealth that accompany these authors and drive their stories. Whether they find this label appropriate, or if they feel their narratives transcend the Western taxonomy of genres and should be situated in their own, renewed territory within their respective literary traditions, only they can say. In any case what we can all do is to provide them with a space where they can express their creativity in order to deal with themes they find interesting in those futuristic coordinates.

Arab science fiction is largely unknown at an international level and so *Arabilious* includes an article by Egyptian author and popularizer Emad El-Din Aysha who provides a historical review of some of the most relevant titles in the history of the genre, underlining, above all, Egyptian contributions. Currently there are only a few works that bring a small number of readers to its shores, though there are a number of initiatives worthy of note that mark a change in direction, opening the door to allowing many Arabic authors to enter the world literary ecosystem.

In 2016 *Iraq+100*, an anthology edited by Iraqi author and director Hassan Blasim, was published by Comma Press. This volume offered a number of Iraqi authors the possibility of imagining their country, through science fiction and fantasy, a century after the military invasion of 2003. In 2019 the same publisher released *Palestine+100*, curated by Palestinian translator Basma Ghalayini. This was an anthology of stories built on the same premise as the other volume. In this version, Palestinian authors explored future visions of their country and people a century after the mass expulsion from their homes in 1948. It must be noted that the same publisher is planning to release another anthology with the same characteristics in 2024. With the title *Egypt+100* it will dig into the future of the country one hundred years after the failed revolution in Tahrir Square. In 2021 Basma Ghalayini co-edited, with author Rasha Abdulhadi, the special edition dedicated to Palestine in the genre magazine *Strange Horizons*.

In 2018 Ian Campbell published *Arabic Science Fiction,* a volume of essays based on his articles relative to various Moroccan and Egyptian science fiction stories, in which he references research of scholars such as Reuven Snir and his text "The Emergence of Science Fiction in Arabic Literature" which appeared in 2000.

Given growing interest in Arab science fiction, it is hardly surprising that important cultural and educational institutions have begun to take notice. In 2013 the Nour Festival in London organised Sindbad Sci-Fi, a meeting with a number of authors and an exhibition about Arab science fiction curated by author Yasmin Khan, and in 2019 the School of

Oriental and African Studies (SOAS) of the University of London dedicated a symposium to them. With the title *Science Fiction Beyond the West: Futurity in African and Asian Contexts*. The interventions of this initiative analysed how imagined futures in the African and Asian contexts influence social themes, explore cultural anxieties, and experiment with alternative possibilities and realities.

Little by little science fiction literature is beginning to gain recognition from critics and the public on the Arabic market thanks not only to initiatives of this kind, but also the visibility provided by important awards. Following this train of thought it is important to mention Noura al-Noman, the female author, translator, and editor from the United Arab Emirates who in 2013 managed to win the Etisalat Children's Books Award for her story *Ajwan*, which she followed with another two books: *Mandan*, and *Saydonia*. This trilogy for young adults, categorised as space opera, discusses themes such as the devastating effects of colonisation, moving of a population and the consequences of forced diaspora.

In 2014 the Iraqi Ahmed Saadawi won the international prize for Arabic narrative (awarded by the Booker Prize Foundation of London with the support of the Emirates Foundation of Abu Dhabi) for *Frankenstein in Baghdad*. It was the first time this prestigious Arabic literary prize was awarded to a work of science fiction with a story set in the Iraqi capital, where a being created from the fragments of people killed in the war sought revenge.

In 2018, Ibrahim Nasralla, a Jordanian-Palestinian writer, won the Arab Booker Prize for *The second war of the dog*, a story where fantasy and science fiction unite to show a dystopian future in an imaginary country without moral values where anything goes, including the buying and selling of human souls.

Within the new wave of dystopian and surreal narrative by writers who are attempting to tackle the chaotic consequences and disappointments of the Arab Spring, it's necessary to mention Basma Abdel Aziz. This female Egyptian writer, psychiatrist and visual artist, published *The Queue* in 2016 which the New York Times compared to *1984* by George Orwell and Franz Kafka's *The Trial*. In 2017 it won her the English PEN translation award. This story takes us to a city with no name in the Middle East where the central authority monopolises power and the citizens have to ask authorisation to carry out every daily task, revealing a kind of sinister authoritarianism, information manipulation and lack of responsibility concerning the defence of the citizens' rights.

Another relevant voice in Arabic Science Fiction is the female Palestinian writer and journalist Ibtisam Azem. Her 2014 story *The book of disappearance*, received great international attention. It proposes a setting where the whole Palestinian population suddenly vanishes. In the same year, Mohamed Rabine published *Otared*, about a future set in the Egyptian capital rendered chaotic by political conflicts and a new drug.

As Darío Marimón García points out, between the end of the twentieth and start of the twenty-first centuries, a new generation of science fiction writers started to appear from scientific sectors, like male Libyan Abdul Hakim Amil al-Tawwil, a nuclear engineer who has for years been writing science fiction stories for Kuwaiti science magazines, and who in 2006 published an anthology of his literary work to date.[1]

---

1 MARIMÓN GARCÍA, DARÍO (2009): "Science Fiction in the Arabic world: approaching its possible origins, general panorama and future of the genre". Essays on science fiction and fantasy fiction: proceedings of the First International Congress of science fiction and fantasy (1, 2008, Madrid).

Probably one of the best known authors outside the Arab world is Ahmed Khaled Tawfik, an Egyptian doctor and author. With over two hundred works he has not only written science fiction and horror in Arabic, but also medical thrillers. His best known book *Utopia*, is a dystopian story published in English by Bloomsbury Qatar Foundation Publishing in 2011, which looks at the life of excesses in a coastal colony in a Cairo of the near future.

Trained in biology, Syrian author Leila Kelani has published various novels including *Journey in the unknown world* in 1975 and *The plants that came to talk* in 2001. We must not forget another Egyptian engineer, Mohamed al-Ashri author of various novels, one of which from 2003 *Halo of light*, can be considered as science fiction because it deals with a new form of life based on silicon. Also from the field of engineering are Saudi Ishraf Ihsan Faqih with various anthologies of hard SF to his name, and Yasser Bahjatt. As an author, Bahjatt has published the novel *Yaqteenya*, in which the Spanish Muslims founded a colony in America, as well as becoming a science fiction ambassador and popularisers of the genre as a sign of society's progress.

We cannot fail to mention an interesting movement connected to the idea of the future in Arab culture: the "Gulf futurism". This term, coined by the American-Kuwaiti multi-discipline artist and author Sophia Al-Maria, delves into the effects of the rapid hyper-modernisation and spreading growth of consumerism and the culture of luxury in the Persian Gulf. An example applied to literature is *The girl who fell to Earth,* a novel with autobiographical undertones published by Al-Maria in 2012 which explores the collision of cultures caused by her family situation.

The aforementioned names are only some of the most important, though not the only ones. A section including all the authors and all their works would need a whole essay, and is not the goal of this project.

The anthology you have in your hands proposes to place a small but important grain of sand in the service of readers all over the world who want to get to know Arabic authors. It was partially planned in autumn 2019 when Francesco Verso, editor of Future Fiction, and I searched land, sea, sky, and air for stories about the future (or futures) directly involving these authors. It has been a hard but very gratifying task that has led us to discover contemporary voices, some directly from countries of the Middle East and North Africa, and some from the diaspora, but all powerful, original, and with singular perspectives on what has happened, the present, and above all, on what is yet to come.

We are convinced that the nine stories in *Arabilious* make up a good example of the new group of contemporary Arab authors: they belong to five female and four male authors from Bahrein, Egypt, Iraq, Lebanon, Jordan, Palestine, and Syria. Two of the stories were written in Arabic, "*A Jaha in the Metaverse*" by Jordanian Fadi Zaghmout and "*Cinnamon Flavour Gum*" by Syrian Maria Dadouch, and were translated for this volume. The other stories were conceived in English, and an author from Bahrain, Nadia Afifi, has contributed two stories: "*Exhibit K*" and "*The Bahrain Underground Bazaar*". It is important to note the particularities of "*Pan-Humanism: Hope and Pragmatics*", because it is the only short story written by four hands, Lebanese Sarah Saab, and Jess Barber. Finally we must thank Emad El-Din Aysha for having contributed in addition to the magnificent article, the story "*Master of the Mediterranean*".

Amongst the recurring themes in these stories are the effects of new technology on Arab society which is deeply rooted in communal life and a long way from the individualism of the West. So, in "*A proposal in the Metaverse*" by Jordanian Fadi Zaghmout, a traditional marriage proposal is carried out in the metaverse, whereas "*Exhibit K*" by Nadi Afifi is about the resuscitation for cultural reasons of people put into cryonic preservation. The author expands this theme in "*The Bahrain underground bazaar*", in which virtual reality cabins allow customers to experience rented lives. Finally, "*A day in the life of Anmar 20X1*" by Palestinian Adulla Moaswes, proposes an intelligent architecture that attempts to make up for the psychological consequences of imposed borders.

Interest for the environment and the devastation perpetrated by global warming appear clearly in the flooded backdrop of "*To New Jerusalem*" by American-Palestinian Farah Kader, in the reconfigured Beirut of "*Pan-humanism Hope and Pragmatics*" by Sara Saab and Jess Barber, and in the baked drought ridden land in "*The standard of Ur*" by the Iraqi Hassan Habulrazzak. In "*Master of the Mediterranean*" by Emad El-Din Aysha, the aforementioned themes mix together to present a future Arab city where something unusual is recycled by it citizens.

Death, absence and loss are strongly present in many of the stories. For example in "*Cinnamon chewing gum*" by Syrian Maria Dadouch people are offered the possibility of prolonging the lives of their descendants through their own assisted suicide by taking a "special" kind of gum, and in the above mentioned stories by Nadia Afifi the protagonists find themselves facing a terrible illness or attempting to adapt to their reborn existence.

Another common thread in almost all of these tales is nostalgia for a past that despite being hard and full of conflicts anchors the characters to their cultural roots and their identity, something that can be seen in the description of the

Nadia Afifi's underground bazaar, or in the childhood memories of the narrators in "*The standard of Ur*" and "*To New Jerusalem*".

The city can be considered as a character in its own right in some of the stories, from the Beirut of "*Pan-humanism: Hope and Pragmatics*", to the partially flooded New York of "*To New Jerusalem*" or the hyper-modern Bahrain of "*The Bahrain Undergrond Bazaar*".

All the aforementioned themes are combined with the rich literary tradition of the Arab population and their history of colonised communities to propose new futuristic alternatives to their existing realities. The stories included in *Arabilious* are full of melancholy, social tensions derived from political conflicts, and from the necessity of taking a step away from the categories and common places established by the West.

We would like to thank the great availability and generosity of Abdulla, Emad, Fadi, Farah, Hassan, Jess, Nadia, Maria and Sarah who participated enthusiastically on this project, and acknowledge the work of the many authors who over the years have defended science fiction with their commitment.

As Yasmin Khan underlined in the quote at the beginning of this introduction, science fiction can become a bridge uniting imagination and innovation in the Arabic world, and can help the rest of the world understand and accept its beauty and specificity. So now, welcome to this anthology; enjoy.

Cristina Jurado
Dubai, 2023

Pan-Humanism: Hope and Pragmatics

by Jess Barber and Sara Saab

Jess Barber splits time between Boston and Los Angeles, where she spends her days (and sometimes nights) building open-source electronics. She is a graduate of the 2015 Clarion Writing Workshop, and her work has appeared in Strange Horizons, Lightspeed, and The Year's Best Science Fiction.

Sara Saab was born in Beirut, Lebanon, and now lives in North London. Her fiction has appeared in Clarkesworld, Shimmer, The White Review, and elsewhere.

1: The Most Hallowed of our Spaces

Amir Tarabi is scrubbing himself down in the misting rooms the first time he meets Mani Rizk.

The mister in Beirut-4 is being upgraded, the zone's residents using Beirut-3's misting rooms on rotation, so it is especially crowded that day. Amir avoids making eye contact with the bathers in adjacent patches with rigorous politeness. At sixteen, he's already spent a hundred personal growth hours thinking about civic decency, appreciates the role of uninterrupted private rituals in fostering social cohesion—

—then someone comes out of the mist and straight into his line of vision, Amir thinks by accident. He *tries* to keep his eyes on what he's doing. The sparse rivulets of soapy water starting in his elbows and armpits are usually an easy bliss to meditate on, how they track down his skin, how they catch and collect on little hairs. Water coalescing from mist doesn't have enough body to drip to the floor. Amir can feel it evaporate at his hips, his thighs, his ankles.

"Excuse me?" says the interrupting someone-who-turns-out-to-be-Mani, and Amir's head lifts before his principles regroup. Her teeth are chattering but she smiles gamely through it. "My patch is really cold. Does that happen?"

"Not that I remember?" he says. "Show me?"

"Sure," she clatters. "Thanks. This way."

He doesn't recall ever being approached by another bather in the mist before. She's naked, so is he, so is everyone. Nudity isn't weird in water-scarce Beirut at the height of summer. Less clothing means less sweat. It's her still-soapy hair that strikes him: so thick that there's two inches of it plastered soaking to her head, which of course means she's nearly at the end of her timeslot. The mist takes a long time to permeate a head of hair.

It's *so* crowded. They weave through an infinity mirror of bathing bodies which fade in the middle distance into a wall of mist. Amir wonders what brought his new friend all the way to his patch when any neighbour would've been glad to help.

"You're from Beirut-4?" he asks.

"The finest of all arbitrary urban planning constructs," she calls back.

At sixteen, Amir doesn't believe in competitive jokes about city zones, just as he doesn't believe in identities constructed in opposition. He doesn't say anything. It doesn't seem the right moment.

Mani finds the four lit wands in the mist that mark the corners of patch 49.

"Cold, right?"

Amir steps solemnly into the center of her patch for a few seconds. The concentrated plume of mist envelops him.

"Feels okay to me?"

Mani shoots him an aghast look, moves into her patch

as Amir steps out. She gives a long-suffering sigh. "Why are they upgrading *our* mister? Beirut-3 needs it more."

"Are you sure you're not physiologically reacting to a new environment?" Amir counters. "All the misters have the same temperature settings."

"Is that so?" Mani says.

"Pretty sure."

She readies a retort, then shakes it off. "Thanks anyway," she says, kneading her hair. "I pulled you away while your mist is running." Sudsy water trickles onto her shoulders.

"That's okay. Enjoy your shower," Amir says, and waves as he leaves her. *Enjoy your shower.* He's vaguely disappointed by the whole exchange for a reason he can't define.

In the airing room, hot blasts of air spread warmth through his chest. This fills him with something like gratitude. He second-guesses whether he might've been cold, before.

"Two degrees lower," says a voice he recognizes.

"Really?" he says after a moment. Now he's vaguely *happy* for reasons he can't place.

"I asked the supervisor. By community agreement, motion passed five years ago, the Beirut-3 misting room is two degrees cooler than default in summer."

"Ah," says Amir. "Good of you to correct a misbelief."

"My pan-humanist agenda's pretty on point," she says. The wry note in her voice doesn't irritate him. "I'm Mani. I live near al-Raouché. Want to do a personal growth hour together?"

Amir doesn't remember what he stammered then, but it must've been affirmative, because the rest of his teenage days have Mani in them, as the water situation worsens, then gets a bit better, then worsens, then stabilizes.

It's a lot of days to have with someone. A lot of staring at the cloudless sky on a blanket from the exposed seabed of al-

Raouché, a lot of synth-protein shawarmas in Hamra, a lot of silent meditative spans huddled in Mani's bed because talking hurts too much with the thirst and their mouths so dry.

But it's also true that all the days in a human life can feel like not enough.

The first time the water situation shows signs of getting better is a Monday. Amir knows this because it's the day for municipal announcements in Beirut-1 through -5. He and Mani are sitting in a seabed cafe in the shadow of al-Raouché. The rock pillar has become a sort of geologic Champs-Élysées, and though the bay has begun to recover from the decades of hyperwarming that dried it out, Beirut Grid have installed a seawall to protect the shops and cafes that went up while water was critically scarce.

"It's oddly beautiful," Amir says to Mani. The seawall is covered with murals depicting water-protection craft, the lighthouse, the rickety old Ferris wheel on the boardwalk. Beyond it, the sea shushes loudly. The sun festers behind the clouds and because Amir and Mani have been through screen-mist they're lounging in just swimming trunks .

Amir rotates his cup and watches bits of tea leaf bob near the bottom. "Do you think it's unethical to celebrate a built environment that's a direct result of water scarcity?" he asks.

Mani looks up from her book: *Pan-Humanism in the Middle East*. It's just come out, and she's been excited to read it because it challenges some of the core arguments of Stella Kadri's *Pan-Humanism: Hope and Pragmatics,* a book of heroic stature for how it butterfly-effected the sociopolitics of the modern world.

"It's not unethical to feel joy if no one's suffering," she says.

"Fish desperate to swim figure eights around al-Raouché could be suffering."

"You have to draw a line where arguments descend into absurdity." She cracks a smile and powers off her book.

"But there's nothing absurd about a healthy marine ecosystem," Amir says. Her pragmatism makes him uneasy. As a life skill it sits uncomfortably against his complete dedication to absolutes: the True, the Good. But it's captivating. It makes her quick to laughter and gracious, even excited, about changing her mind.

Mani gulps her tea. "Still hot. So now I've burned my tongue worrying about the fish." She glances down. "Didn't I turn that off?" Her book's flashing a notification. So is her watch. So are her shades.

Amir blows on his tea before he sips. "On override? Must be important."

They read the message, heads hovering together. It's from the municipality. *Beirut Water pilot. First sectors, random pick: Beirut-4, Beirut-9. Water reconnected via mains for 24hrs from 2PM. OK: taps, showers, hoses. Use judgment: industrial electronics.*

It takes a moment to sink in.

"Wait. Are you kidding?"

"I had no idea they were ready to try," Mani says.

They're both gathering their things, tapping over a tabclose, standing. "Warsaw managed to run a water supply off a condensation system for a week," Amir says. "But this is *Beirut*."

"So what if it is?" Mani says. "Beirut is superb! Beirut has water!"

They're skipping along the stairs to the boardwalk. A louder murmur than the sea is rising from the seabed cafe: the municipality message spreading.

They reach Mani's house in record time. It's a hot day and Amir is itching from sweat and screen residue with an urgency he's never felt before.

"Mom? There's water!" Mani shouts into the dark house.

"No one," says Amir.

"Ah, she's got an hour of cross-skilling this afternoon."

"Should we wash our hands?" Amir pants, chasing Mani up the stairs.

"Don't be ridiculous. Have to go all the way." She opens a door in the hall. "In here."

Amir follows her. She's planted in front of a bone-dry shower stall. The showerhead is impossibly shiny. There's still a bit of plastic wrapping on it. It's an antique, but brand new.

"It's nearly two o'clock."

"Are they going to be able to do this?"

"Trust, Amir. Trust."

"Do you think it might even be heated?"

Mani, scooting out of her swimming costume , raises her eyebrows at him till he shoves his down too. "I bet it is." She reaches into the shower stall and twists a handle. It screeches with disuse.

They wait.

At exactly two, their ears fill with the furious sound of a rainstorm. Then their own whooping. Mani bounds in without testing the temperature, makes a shrill sound. "It's warming up!" She reaches out and grabs Amir's arm. Her grip raises goosebumps. "Come on, get in!"

He does. It's the most sublime thing he's ever felt. He puts his hands flat on the wet tiles and closes his eyes under a hammering of water.

"How long can we stay in here?" He manages not to choke. Such a quantity of water is coursing down his face and onto his tongue.

"We're being good by sharing. Let's not get out for a while," Mani says. "Are you crying?"

"Yes!" He opens his eyes to look at her but her face is blurry-wet. "Are you?"

"That's private," Mani says. But she wraps her arms around his waist, her belly against his flank, and rests her forehead on his cheek. Their bodies are slippery and warm. Amir hears himself make a purring noise. "Oh. Wow."

"Yeah."

"Not like the mist," he says.

"No. Totally different."

Sharing a patch is encouraged in the misting rooms. They've done this many times. They wash each other's backs and argue about what true pan-humanism might look like. It's pleasurable. But this—private, warm, untimed, all this water sheeting down—is a whole different register of existence.

"I think I should tell you," Mani says, "that I'm thinking about sex."

Amir opens one eye to look at her, can only see the top of her head against his cheek. "Me, too," he says, almost but not totally redundantly. Mani's got a good view.

They have *almost* so many times, but never actually. This moment feels ripe, so very theirs. But it's also the wrong moment.

"Water, though, Mani! Mindfulness. Presence. This."

"Of course," she says.

"We might never be able to have this again."

"We might never have any given thing again," Mani says, the pedantic one for a change.

"But all this water," he says.

"No, you're right," says Mani, hushed in the hypnotic roar of the shower. "All this water."

The Beirut Water pilot is considered only a partial success;

it isn't repeated again for almost two years. By then Mani has left. Amir will remember different selections of things from the day of the pilot depending on how hot or cold his thoughts are, but he'll cap the memory with this, every single time: the fond way Mani slides her hand against his drenched ribs under the flow of hot water before she entirely lets him go.

Amir sleeps poorly the night before the university assignments are due to be announced. He knows but does not *know*-know that he will get into Beirut and Environs, his first choice. His grades are excellent. He's done twenty per cent more personal growth hours than required—he *likes* doing them—and his civic engagement score is the highest ever for Beirut-3's Academy. But he's still nervous. When his watch buzzes at four in the morning, he is startled awake: BEIRUT AND ENVIRONS FUTURIST COLLEGE, UTOPIAN PHILOSOPHY STREAM.

He taps over the notification to Mani with a string of exclamation points, his foggy enthusiasm-slash-relief dampened only slightly when she doesn't respond right away. Mani's grades are stellar but her civic engagement score's not great. She'd wanted Pan-Humanist Polytechnic but Amir has a sinking feeling she's been assigned to College of the Near East.

He composes a fortifying speech in his head as he gets ready, complete with references to the most famous pan-humanist thinkers who'd attended Near East and their contributions to society. Near East is a great school, and it's half an hour closer to Beirut and Environs by bullet than Pan-Humanist Polytechnic. Mani will do amazing things wherever she goes.

Amir is fifteen minutes early for the morning's personal growth session. They've only just opened the doors to the

Reflection Center, a handful of early risers filter in under the kaleidoscopic arches, there is a quiet murmuring of conversation as they set up mats and blankets on the centuries-old stone floor. Mani is already there waiting for him, sitting cross-legged on her mat, gripping her hands together so tight that her fingers are white to the knuckle. Amir is brought up short.

"Mani?" he asks, uncertain.

Wordlessly, she raises her wrist for him to see, the notification still up on the watch screen: INTL UNIVERSITY FOR HUMANISM, MOGADISHU, GLOBAL PROGRESS.

Amir feels his heart go ka-thunk. Global Progress at IUH is . . . he'd thought about applying, more as a lark than anything, but they only accept three students per year, from the entire world, and he never thought . . .

"Wow," he says, dropping down next to her, voice low so it won't echo. "Wow, Mani, that's—I didn't even know you were going to *apply,* that's—amazing. That's so amazing. I'm so, so proud of you," he says, and even means it.

Mani's face is complicated with emotions, flickering by too quickly for Amir to properly catalog them, happy-sad-excited-nervous. "It's far away," she says.

"It's *exciting,*" he corrects. "Mogadishu, can you even imagine! Maybe I could visit you, one time." This is unlikely, and they both know it. Mogadishu's not on a clean air travel vector with Beirut yet. He'd have to do two months of civic engagement and a month of personal growth to balance taking a dirty flight for leisure. Mani musters a smile anyway.

"I'd love that," she says. In the center of the room, today's meditation guide is setting up at the podium. The overhead heaters have been switched on, spreading the scent of the cedar beams throughout the space. Mani bumps Amir's shoulder with her own. Her smile builds into something a little more true. "Come on, though. We both know you'll be too busy changing the world to think of me at all."

2: The Mechanism, A Worthwhile Trade

It's not that Mani's right, because of course Amir thinks of her. He thinks of her every single day, at least he did at first, but when the water starts coming back to Beirut and Amir gets swept up in the civic spirit, in the new swell of hope. He switches out of Utopian Philosophy the day after he helps a volunteer group install a kinetic walkway on the university's main green—they expect to be able to clean-power the quad's lamps for two hours each night—and enrolls in Urban Design. The idea of regeneration-planning the city is wedged deep under his skin.

After graduation he walks into a competitive apprenticeship with Beirut Grid, where he meets Rafa, who's working on the Bekaa Valley's poetry microcity and in the capital on up-skill, and Ester, a third generation Beiruti whose grandmother led the rights movement for domestic workers at the turn of the century. They all fall for each other almost simultaneously.

He's twenty-two. He's got an apartment on al-Manara. Through his kitchen window, the lighthouse illuminates the brushstroke sea foam of the Mediterranean, and every time Amir Tarabi sees it he says a silent word of hope for the sea, for it to have body and swell with muscle forever. He remembers his conversation with Mani about the fish, imagines a day in the future when they'll wade into the surf and see entire schools, silver and bronze and fleeting, with their own eyes.

Amir's at work late when his watch buzzes. Rafa and Ester. *Let us in, we're at the door to Research-4.*

He limps down the hall on pins-and-needles in his feet. The recollection that they'd planned a dinner date for tonight—for an hour ago—wallops him right before he releases the door.

Rafa and Ester don't usually band together against Amir, but here they are, standing side by side wearing exactly the same expression, and it's not *we're so glad to see you.*

Ester raises a package and Amir smells food.

"I don't remember *ever* blowing off a date with Amir when I worked at the Grid," Ester says pointedly to Rafa.

"Hmm, Ester," Rafa replies theatrically. "Is that because you were respectful of his time and attention? Because you understood that interpersonal relationships require careful cultivation?"

"I'm *so* sorry," Amir squeaks, letting them in, putting a hand out for their coats. "Can I explain what happened? Not an excuse, just context."

Ester looks at Rafa. Rafa looks at Ester. Both of them look skeptically at Amir.

"You guys, I'm sorry. Do you remember my Crowd-grow thing?"

"Where you wanted to foster-out eco-boosted flowers around the neighbourhood?" asks Rafa. "You told us about it last month."

"Right," says Amir. "We found out today the bio team managed to get a couple of shoots synthesizing air pollutants in the lab. Mesilla asked me to put together a grant application for the project. If it gets funded she wants me to lead the research team."

Amir is fortunate that both his partners know what this means to him. Their faces soften.

"Nice. I knew Mesilla would come around," Ester says. "You still don't get to flake on dates."

In a deserted Beirut Grid kitchenette, Amir fetches plates and Rafa piles seasoned eggplant casserole onto them. While they eat Amir projects stained photos of cross-sectioned saplings onto a wall, and Rafa and Ester *mmm* through his commentary for a few minutes, until Rafa says,

"Amir, love, it's nine and you're still using words like 'floral load.'"

"Good point, Rafa," Ester says. "Amir, hand over projector control."

The projection cuts to the backdrop of his favorite immersion strategy game.

"I've got dessert," Rafa says. He produces a huge bag of caramel chews and a bottle of whiskey. They clear some space.

"Ooh," Ester says, confirming a glance-down-pause setting. "We need to be able to snack."

"Oh *no,*" Amir says. "This never goes well. It's an *immersion* game."

"Shush," Rafa says. "It's destined to be a drunk immersion game."

Their love is like this, comfortable and forgiving of Amir's faults. Then, at the beginning of summer, Ester breaks up with Rafa and Amir—no hard feelings, just different needs, different takes on life. It's not that it doesn't hurt. Amir and Rafa spend several days moping in each other's laps, swapping sympathy cuddles, but Amir has always believed what pan-humanist theory says: that love is respect and collaboration held together with radical acceptance, freely gained and lost.

Amir tells himself to take comfort in this, and does his best to keep an open heart.

The Future Good conference in Hanoi is the biggest of its kind, twelve academic streams and full air travel exemption. Amir and Rafa apply for spots every year and never get them, until they do. They're giddy on the flight over: neither of them gets to leave Beirut often, and they've certainly never had a reason to travel by air together.

They attend the welcome address then spend the allotted cultural hours in the Old Quarter sitting on low stools with their knees knocking together, feeding each other quail egg bánh bao. Rafa's old advisor is leading a Q&A session on arts micro-cities, but Rafa and Amir lose track of time strolling the banks of the Red River hand in hand. Once they've missed that, there's no reason to go back to the hotel, so they stay out till three in the morning sampling the sticky rice wine which everyone *tries* to warn them is stronger than it tastes.

The next morning's reclamation technologies forum is something of an accident.

They're trying—oh, Amir is almost too embarrassed to admit it. They're *trying* to find breakfast, and Rafa spies a cute ambiguously-gendered human with multicolored hair and a dapper three-piece suit sneaking out of one of the conference rooms, arms full of coffee cups and muffins. Amir and Rafa are *hungry,* so they creep into the back, sights set on the buffet table lining the rear wall, and there is Mani Rizk, making her way to the front podium.

Amir's entire body floods with adrenaline. He grabs Rafa by the cuff of his sleeve and steers him to one of the chairs. He's trying to be stealthy but Rafa is mumbling confused protests around a coffee machine and Mani sees them, of *course* she does, and her face goes from taken aback to pleased. And then she does a pretty good job of pretending she didn't see Amir, because she's got a lecture to deliver.

Rafa stares at Amir in confusion for about a minute before his eyebrows go up in a particularly knowing manner. He spends the rest of the lecture elbowing Amir any time Mani says something brilliant, which is about every thirty seconds.

"*So?*" Rafa asks, delighted, when the lecture is over and they're waiting at the back of a densely knotted crowd. "Who is she, eh? Political rival? Academic crush? Long lost lover?"

"*No,*" protests Amir, a little too loudly for the enclosed space. "She's just—a friend. We were friends, when we were young. That was all."

If nothing else, Mani seems at least as eager to see him as he is to see her: her attention keeps sliding away from whoever she's talking with, darting to Amir again and again. He smiles, catching her eye, and spreads his hands in an awkward gesture that he hopes will convey both *hi* and *I'll wait.* As soon as the crowd thins enough for her to break away she does so, inching her way to Amir and Rafa with a string of apologies and excuses.

"Amir," she says, and half-tackles him in a hug.

She's round and solid and *small*—it's weird, Amir hadn't hit his growth spurt until he was eighteen, and in his memory they're still like that, him looking up. Now Mani barely comes up to his collarbone. He wraps arms that feel oddly long and lanky around her shoulders and holds her tight.

When she finally lets go her eyes look suspiciously bright, but that might just be the ceiling lights. "I didn't know you were coming to my talk," she says.

"It was kind of an accident," Amir admits.

Beside him, Rafa groans. "Don't *tell* her that!" He turns to Mani. "What he means to say is, he wanted to surprise you. And your lecture was phenomenal."

"I'm not going to *lie* to her," says Amir, affronted. "About the surprise, I mean. Your lecture *was* phenomenal. I didn't know you'd been studying hydrophobic materials."

"I'm part of a water reclamation forum at IUH," says Mani, and then, to Rafa, "and I've known Amir too long to expect flattery. I'm Mani."

"Rafa Zarkesian. I consult on architecture projects for art spaces in Beirut."

"Rafa's my boyfriend," says Amir. It seems important to mention.

"Oh, I thought I recognized you! I've seen your picture on Amir's stream. How long—"

"Mx Rizk?" cuts in a voice over Mani's shoulder. "I'm so sorry to intrude, but—"

"No, no, of course," says Mani. "Sorry, I really should—"

"Yes, of course," says Amir. "It was good to see you, Mani, I—"

"Tonight," she interrupts, "after closing remarks. There's that gallery installation, the interactive city grid? I haven't been able to see it yet. If you have time, maybe the three of us . . ."

They've got a pre-dawn flight back to Beirut; they'd planned to get to bed early and had contemplated skipping the closing remarks entirely.

"That would be wonderful," says Rafa. "We wouldn't miss it."

That night, it rains in Hanoi, just a light, champagne-fizz mist, but it's enough to lend a celebratory attitude to the entire city. They find Mani waiting for them outside the installation's entrance, a crown of water droplets clinging to her hair, reflecting a riot of blinking, changeable light. Amir grips Rafa's hand a little harder.

"We got lucky," Mani says, squinting as she tilts her face upward, holding out a cupped palm as if to collect water there. "Good closing note for the conference."

"Lucky," echoes Amir, feeling a little dazed.

Rafa bumps his shoulder against Amir's. "Come on, you two," he says, already attached. "Let's go in."

The installation is a concept city rendered in one-fifti-eth scale in shimmering interactive holograms and delicate print-resin latticework. The space isn't enclosed, and the scrim of the rain occasionally does glitchy things to the pro-jections that make Amir groan in solidarity with the event planners. Rafa and Mani are both charmed, however, and Amir can't help but be delighted by their delight. He gets video of the support cables of a projected suspension bridge twining around Mani's ankles, insistent and loving as a cat. They take turns decorating Rafa with sprigs of star-like flow-ers in the constructed wetlands section.

At one point, Amir is walking sandwiched between the two of them, face craned up to ogle the dazzling phyllotactic arch-way they're underneath. Rafa reaches down to twine his fingers with Amir's, and, after a moment that might be hesitation, on the other side Mani reaches down and does the same. Amir can feel his own heartbeat in his palms and he's sure Mani and Rafa must be able to as well, but neither of them says a thing.

Afterward, they make promises about staying in better contact. There's a conference in Mogadishu, only six months away; it's not a perfect fit for his research, but maybe Amir can swing an invite. It's ridiculous, really, that Amir hasn't yet seen Mani's new city, Mani's new life. Mani's so busy—they're all so busy, but they can message more, at least. Maybe even holochat sometimes. They work in related fields, after all; it's their responsibility to foster international communi-cation and collaboration. Plus, they *miss* each other. There's no reason to fall so out of touch.

They say all this, and mean it. But, well. Life.

3: Each Brick Laid Thousands of Times Over

The lab at Beirut Grid successfully demonstrates quanti-ty ecoboosting in model organisms two weeks before Amir turns twenty-eight, which is a pretty good early birthday present as far as he's concerned. To celebrate Mesilla takes Amir to the botanical garden in Rmeil to evaluate options for the Crowdgrow pilot; Hanne from New Projects tags along.

The conservatory curator herself gives them a guided tour. She leads them down dense green walkways, extols the growth patterns of crawler vines and Chouf evergreens, both commendably hardy species and survivors of the worst of the water scarcity. Mesilla seems invested—she examines a potted evergreen the curator has handed her and sinks a finger into the soil—but Hanne is paying zero attention, cleaning up her notifications on Impulse or something. Then, out of nowhere Hanne blurts out,

"Oh, Mesilla. They just announced funds for a world-first Wet City implementation."

The crinkly cellophane of the potted evergreen goes still. The curator says, "Anything else I can show you?" into the silence; Amir babbles about high-altitude crawler vines. They move on to another greenhouse.

Later, in line for lunch, Amir waits for Mesilla to pick his brain. He's all but decided he wants to try ecoboosting crawler vines, but wouldn't mind talking it through.

"So," Mesilla says as soon as they've found a sunny patch of grass on Achrafieh green for a picnic, "There's a Wet City funding opportunity? When's the deadline?"

"One month," says Hanne. "Not much time to put together a proposal."

Amir puffs out his breath, struggling to rearrange his thoughts. "Has anyone proven the water reclamation wings would work at that scale? Wasn't that the sticking point in Colson and Smith's paper?"

Hanne jabs the chunk of carrot on the end of her fork at

Amir. "Right. But the All People funds were greenlit on the back of a rebuttal slash instruction manual by—" Hanne's eyes blink away as she navigates Impulse. "By Sameen Jaladi at IUH Mogadishu." The name of Mani's school fills Amir with a mixture of possessiveness and pride.

Amir can think of twenty reasons to be wary: the technical challenge of large-scale moisture collection, yes, but also overheating the built habitat, uncontrollable wet seasons, mold and mosquitos and respiratory conditions. That's not to mention his immediate questions around clean-powering the wings and purging waste bays. He puts his sandwich in its basket and turns to Mesilla.

"It's a lot of resources toward an unproven concept. We'd have to divert money and energy we could spend in demonstrably useful directions," he says. *Like on Crowdgrow,* he doesn't say.

"But in *theory,*" Mesilla says. "Every metropolis could be a little green oasis. Latticed condensation wings, clean water from the air. Theoretically, no shortages ever again."

She unwraps a bit more sandwich in a studied way: bean protein fillet in yogurt and mint sauce, her usual. "Can someone get me the Jaladi paper and the bid guidelines?"

Amir's already poring through Impulse. He taps the documents over to Mesilla with two hard blinks. "They're with you."

They walk back to the Beirut Grid offices talking about Amir's birthday plans—Joud is taking him on an overnight bullet to Damascus; their first trip together as a couple—but the lunch conversation is still humming under his skin.

Two days later, when Mesilla pulls Amir and Hanne aside and asks them to put together a Wet City bid, it doesn't surprise him.

It's a hot day with a really crappy clean air index. Everyone has been permitted to stay home but a few of them came in anyway, including Amir, because his apartment was so hot he feared he might melt into his armchair. The heat reminds him of sitting in a seabed café with Mani, which of course reminds him of the Future Good conference with Mani, which takes Amir's thoughts nowhere helpful at all.

The Impulse note arrives from Mesilla in two parts. The first, short, buzzes at his wrist and pings urgently in his display. It's to Amir and Hanne, two words: *We won!*

He expects excitement but feels only bone-tiredness.

The second part of Mesilla's note is a travel itinerary on wider distribution. The subject line makes Amir's body do weird things: *Academics from IUH Mogadishu.* He taps it open on his wrist, as if he needs to see this in physical space, and sure enough:

Jaladi, Sameen
Proctor, Trevor
Gupta, Jan-Helga
Rizk, Mani

"Shit," he croaks. His side of the office is empty. He can hear the descending xylophone of the bullet zipping along its girders through the open window, and nearer, a heat-oppressed bird call that sounds more tired than he does.

He blinks up his conversation thread with Mani. Their last exchange: *Happy new year!* from her to him, half a year ago; *Happy new year!!* from him to her a couple hours later, and since then, nothing. He winces.

Beirut???? he taps over.

Mani's response is almost instant. *Leave in a week.*

!!! Amir sends. His belly is one big knot.

Took the effusive punctuation straight out of my mouth, she replies.

Amir wrangles his way into airport chaperon duty for the IUH academics. At Future Good, running into Mani had been a sudden shock; the week he waits for her plane to arrive his nerves are like a leaky faucet. He can't eat properly but finds himself stocking his pantry with everything he remembers Mani loving: carob molasses, salted pilinuts, a Bekaa Valley Merlot, cashew feta cheese. Joud tries to season a stew with the good cinnamon sticks Amir picked up at al-Raouché market for spiced tea and Amir won't let them.

"I'm saving those," Amir says, guiltily filing away that there should be a Joud-him-Mani dinner involving cinnamon sticks. He doesn't know what's wrong with him. The plane from Mogadishu, oblivious and probably flying over Independent Greenland on other business, is killing him.

Then he's at the airport and his Impulse tells him the flight from Mogadishu has arrived safely. Mani has sent him her Impulse geo, which means he can tell exactly when she's walking through customs and toward the public area.

He distracts himself by trying to calculate how long it's been since they've seen each other using mental math. His Impulse helper picks up on his saccades. *You seem to be working something out. Can I help?* Amir moans and blinks it away. He finishes the calculation—1,513 days—but now he can barely breathe. Then the arrivals door pistons up to reveal a column of passengers. He sees Mani in the throng, and she sees him back.

It's not the moment he's been imagining. Mani is engrossed in conversation with her colleagues. She weaves them toward Amir and he wants to hug her but the fact that he's on official duty—that there are three field-pioneering academics he's never met, studying him—roots him to the spot.

"Hi," Mani says.

"Hi," Amir says. Not *wow, you and me in Beirut, like when we were seventeen.* Which is what he's thinking.

"Sameen, Trevor, Helga, Amir," Mani says, and then there's a blur and they're all on the bullet in the private compartment Amir booked and everyone is staring out the window at the city they've missed or never seen before, and the conversation turns to how wonderfully Beirut will function as a Wet City.

He tries not to catch Mani's eye too much, but when he does she gives him a conspiratorial smile he remembers. He thinks of the wine and the cheese. They'll get loads of time together later.

Except, the next day Mesilla kicks off the Wet City stuff in earnest and Amir and Mani start to argue. A lot.

In some ways it's not new. They'd argued as kids, the minutiae of pan-humanist theory over hot black tea: whether animals deserved more pronounced protection than plants, whether population control was ever justified, whether power should in all cases decentralize in the direction of local communities.

The stakes are different now. *They* 'are different. The worst of the arguments take place during project meetings, in front of Hanne and Caveg and the rest of the team. Amir leaves meeting after meeting feeling battered. The way Mani seems to have a reassuring study on hand to refute each of his worries makes him clench his jaw in a very uncivic way. He's so embarrassed by this incessant jaw clenching he grows his beard out to hide it.

They avoid casual conversation for the better part of two weeks. Amir starts to hate going to work, which has never happened before. Then, one Monday, Mani stops at Amir's station, and gets close to see if he's working in Impulse. He can smell her perfume, mineral and saline and only the slightest bit sweet.

"Help me draft an advisory? If you're not busy?" she asks. She lifts a satchel. "I brought us tea from kiosk auntie downstairs."

"Advisory?" Amir's immediately on edge. "Do you need planning language in it? Can Caveg help?"

Mani's eyebrows come down. "I don't really need planning language in it. I just miss doing things together. I thought there'd be a lot more of that."

"Yeah," Amir says, and stands to follow. He remembers following her that first time, in the misting rooms. He doesn't understand himself. He's been waiting to have Mani back for a decade—not a vague wistfulness, but an active full-body sort of waiting, if he's honest with himself. And now she's right here, and he can't bring himself to speak to her without getting upset. The funny thing is that he's not even angry at her. It's something more like bedazzlement. She's a sun that blasts his vision into afterimages.

"Or," Amir says in the corridor, "we could go to our old café? It won't be too busy right now."

Mani nods decisively. "Let's go. Sameen will happily take the kiosk auntie tea."

The bullet ride is mainly Mani pointing out new art installations and green spaces and Amir telling her what year they were built and why. He's good at this. He does almost all of them without Impulse, but confesses when he has to look one up. Mani gives him grief for not knowing them *all* by heart.

"Everyone told me, *oh, Amir, Beirut Grid's own whiz kid.* A sort of city-planning savant. I guess I expected more," she teases.

"No one said that," Amir says. "And even if they did, IUH has given you impossible expectations."

"Pan-humanism is all about realizing a civilizational system that game theory would say is impossible, right?"

"Right," says Amir. "But there's plain old pan-humanist theory impossible and then there's IUH Mogadishu impossible."

The bullet slows and stops beside their old café. They go down the boardwalk to their usual table, tap across an order of tea, and settle into their respective chairs. "Wow," says Amir.

"Swap adult clothes for swimming costumes and shave the beard and it could be a decade ago."

Amir lifts their order of tea off a tray bot. "Were we that familiar with each other? Hard to believe."

Mani takes her glass from him. "Oh yeah. We were ridiculous. Like one person in two bodies, back then."

Amir is startled in a way that melts him into himself, like his chest is swallowing the rest of him, swallowing his words. Mani has always been the forthright one, but they both know he's more sentimental, and he's afraid that if he says anything now it will be too much.

"You don't like the beard?" he manages.

Mani reaches across and strokes his cheek against the grain. "I don't *not* like it," she says.

Amir shakes his head at her. She withdraws her hand. He'd forgotten how *transparent* they were to each other. Are, to each other.

"How's Rafa?" Mani says, stirring her tea.

"We broke up last year." He doesn't bother waving it off. Mani will know it was a big deal.

Mani's silent a bit, then: "I just ordered you a glass of ʿarak."

Amir laughs and puts his head on his arms. "It's only two o'clock, but thank you." Seagulls croon from the frames of the yellow beach umbrellas. "This Wet City thing, Mani," he starts. Doesn't know how to finish.

"You don't believe in it," says Mani.

Amir grimaces. "That obvious?"

"No." This should be reassuring, but Mani is turning her teacup in slow circles, not meeting Amir's eyes. "Amir-with-his-heart-not-in-it works with more passion than most humans on their best days. But I can tell."

This should also be reassuring. Instead Amir feels irritation spiking in his chest. "I've spent every moment of my workday for the past six days chasing down permit documentation for an experimental metallofoam that's going to be used in less than two percent of the load-bearing struts of the wing structure," he says. "It's not exactly how I envisioned my career path. But I'm doing it. It's not fair to call me out for lack of enthusiasm."

"I wasn't calling you out," says Mani. "I think you're doing good work."

"Yeah," says Amir. The 'arak comes. He plucks it off the tray bot and sets it next to his teacup, aligning them carefully side by side. He can tell Mani is waiting for him to say something else. He shouldn't. He should try to steer the conversation back towards safety. "Do you remember," he says, "the Crowdgrow project I told you about during the Future Good conference?"

"You were really excited about it," Mani says. "It seemed promising."

"It was. The closed-room tests showed a fifteen percent improvement in air quality, and we had almost a thousand households signed up as testers. We've applied for continuation funding every open cycle since. Not a lot—just enough for a pilot study. Less than we spend in administrative overhead on the Wet City project every week."

"But no luck?" asks Mani.

"But no luck," agrees Amir.

"Amir," says Mani, but there's too much pity in the way she says his name.

"I know what you're thinking," Amir says. "That it would be a waste. That Wet City is a better use of resources."

"Yes," says Mani. "I do think that." The way she says this could have been kind, but it isn't.

"You're always so sure of yourself," says Amir. The way he says this could have been a compliment, but it isn't. "Is it ego?"

"Is it jealousy?" Mani shoots back.

Amir feels that familiar muscle in his jaw clench. He takes a careful, measured sip of ʿarak, as if that will hide it. "If this goes wrong—" he begins, once he's sure his voice will come out steady.

"Oh, please," interrupts Mani. "You're going to tell me to be afraid of trying something really big, really innovative, because there's a chance we'll end up looking like fools? Now *that's* ego."

"It's not about *personal reputation*," Amir says. "It's about the wasted money, the time, the emotional investment—do you know how demoralizing a project like this can be for a community if it fails—"

"It won't fail."

"You can't know that."

"We've done all the tests and simulations and proof-of-concept models we can, Amir. The only way to be any more sure is to let someone else go first, and I'm not willing to do that."

"Ego," says Amir.

"So what," Mani snaps, sounding genuinely angry now, "we'd all be better off staying in our backyards planting mutant daisies? Grow up, Amir. You have the chance to work on something that really, actually matters here, and you're too scared to take it."

If it were Amir, he would regret such harsh words immediately, start falling all over himself to apologize before the sting had a chance to land.

But it's Mani. And Mani always says what she means.

Amir looks down at the now-empty glass cradled in his fingers. "It's getting late," he says. "We should probably be getting back."

Mani stands, the legs of her chair protesting loudly against the concrete. "We get this chance—" she stops. "I can't understand why you're making it so hard."

He should argue. Instead, he orders another ʿarak, and doesn't let himself watch her walk to the bullet station.

4: That Each of Us Invests The Labor

It's not that Amir and Mani stay angry a whole year and a half. Something that dire would have spurred Amir to action, forced him to have the trembly, awkward conversation that showed them the way back to exchanges of essay clippings and meandering debates and maybe even limb-jumble lie-downs after a gigantic dinner cooked together.

They are not *angry*: they are too intelligent for anger, Amir thinks, or too proud. They're just *hardened* to each other. Their words bounce, too few being absorbed. Their lunches together have one too many silences that call for a new conversation thread, and when congratulations are due—as when the first wing is drone-dropped into place at Martyrs' Square and measurements show promising vapor transfer into the condensation bays at the base—their hugs are guarded and lacking substance.

The Wet City project hits miraculously few snags, but

once or twice Amir catches a design flaw that makes Mani give him a deep, reckoning look.

"I'm just doing some calculations in Impulse," Amir says. "The Beirut-3 east wing might not come out inwardly reflective the way we want, with the new bug-in-amber angled like that?" *Bug-in-amber* is their shorthand for the art pieces they'll embed in each translucent wing, one of Amir's favorite streams of the project. He taps across his calculations.

"Whizkid," is all Mani says, and Amir almost asks if she wants to grab dinner with him after work. He doesn't. He gets better at finding flaws, though. There are times when flaws are all he sees.

Post-water-crisis Beirut is mesmerizing, boisterous street markets by day and elaborate street parties by night.

Amir and Joud meet every couple of weeks to trawl the artisan quarter in Nouveau Centre-Ville, Amir on the lookout for sustainable art references for the much larger bug-in-amber pieces to come, Joud hoping to enrich their collection of silk and brocade Lebanese abayas. They are especially taken by androgynous styles that combine an embroidered abaya tunic with a shirwal bottom. They stroke the parchment packets, their fingers lingering on the teardrop calligraphy of the artisan's sigil. The two of them often return to Amir's apartment with towering ice cream cones, and Joud tells him what they've learned about tonight's artisan on Impulse, and they have the sort of voracious, aching sex that comes after absence.

"How is Mani?" Joud asks tonight, nestled against the hollow of Amir's chest. Joud frequently asks about Mani. They *know,* but their affection for Amir is so confident, so stable, that the question can come right after intimacy and carry no trace of malice or envy.

"Today she proposed a walkway up the side of the sea-facing wings for a view of the sunset," Amir says. "And yesterday she gave a site tour to a delegation that arrived two days early from Singapore."

Joud hums in appreciation. They always do. Joud loves expansively, navigating a multitude of relationships with a grace and wholeheartedness that makes Amir feel he's never absorbed a moment of personal growth.

"You don't have to indulge me, you know," Amir says. He presses three fingertips against the place where Joud's temple meets soft brown hair, scratches them there tenderly. "You and I have been in each other's lives for two years and I've never been—I mean, Mani's always been—"

Joud stills his lips with their cheek. "It doesn't bother me, darling. What I figure is some people stand beside each other, and some people end up locked together," Joud laces their own hands tight, to the knuckles. "And I don't think the latter is better."

"You're right, love," Amir says to Joud, who smells like green branches and clay and sex. In that moment the appellation feels miraculous and genuine on his tongue. "In many ways it's worse."

There are times when hitting the forecast Wet City launch date seems like a pipe dream, but as more and more pieces slot into place, it starts to become attainable, and then an unavoidable reality. Twenty hyper-efficient months after Hanne's distracted aside in the conservatory, the first wings come online; the engineers begin their final stress tests; the notion of a citywide festival around the launch begins to coalesce. And then, with three and a half months to the launch date, Mesilla calls Amir into her office.

Two of their artists won't have their bugs-in-amber finished by the festival and Amir's been heading up the effort to ensure their temporary prototypes are materially similar enough for the engineers to work with; he assumes this is what Mesilla wants to talk about. Instead he's greeted by a stranger. "Amir," Mesilla says, "I wanted you to meet one of my oldest colleagues: Adah Bertonneau."

Adah Bertonneau is even taller than Amir, with impressive cheekbones and two-handed clasp handshake. "A pleasure to finally meet you," Adah says, their accent a rich, rolling thing Amir can't quite place.

Amir smiles, puzzled. "Finally?"

"Read your Crowdgrow grant application five years ago now," says Adah. "Told myself I'd make Mesilla introduce us if I ever made it to this part of the globe. And here I am."

"Oh." Amir resists the inclination to try to look up Adah on Impulse—he's still not very good at interfacing with it discreetly. "Well, unfortunately, we haven't had the opportunity to prove out the research, but I hope that one day—"

"Mx Tarabi," interrupts Adah. "That is, of course, precisely why I'm here to talk to you."

Adah Bertonneau, it turns out, works at the Nantes Center for Naturalist Studies. The Center is neither large nor prestigious (Amir gives up and looks it up on Impulse), but their work seems well-respected enough, and a few of their recent papers have appeared in journals Amir would have once given his eyeteeth to be published in. Adah's lab is new, getting off the ground with an *extremely* generous grant from France Centrale, and it seems, more or less, that they're looking for ways to spend it.

"One must make a splash early," says Adah, peering at Amir seriously over the rim of their teacup. "We're frontloading, trying to get several programs up and running right out the door. Not all of them will work out in the long term, of course, but I'd guarantee funding for the full two-year period you requested, regardless of the findings. Between you and me, though? I have this . . . call it a premonition, that what you've proposed is going to work."

Of course it's a dream come true, and of course the timing couldn't be worse.

"I wish I could tell you to take your time making a decision," continues Adah, "but the start date's in a month, and I'm afraid it's not flexible." They want to do the study with a particular crawler vine, Adah explains, and its cuttings are most viable in the fall. One week, and they'll need a yes or no, "else there won't be enough time to get the paperwork in order, you understand." Amir understands. Hands are shaken. Mesilla walks Amir out.

"Take the rest of the day," she says. "I—well, I don't know whether to say I'm sorry or congratulations. I know it's a lot all at once."

Amir very nearly just asks her to tell him what to do, and she seems to read this on his face. "We can talk it over tomorrow, if you need. But sleep on it, before you start cataloging opinions."

Amir nods. It's smart. Mesilla's always smart. He goes to his office, gathers his things, does his best to slip out unnoticed.

Except he runs into Mani waiting for the elevator.

"Hey," she says, smiling a little awkwardly, that try-hard friendliness. Then she spots his messenger bag. "Headed out?"

It's not even ten in the morning. Amir hits the down button again—the Grid's elevators are vintage, which is a cute way of saying unbearably slow. The doors are mirrored; Amir read somewhere that mirroring elevator doors reduced complaints about wait times, because people got carried away admiring themselves. He wonders if it's true. He hopes it's not. He thinks it probably is.

"Mani," he says, "I'm quitting."

Mani's reflection stares at him.

The doors bing open.

Amir steps into the elevator; Mani takes an extra second to step in after him.

"*Explain,*" Mani says. "*Now*? Are you serious?"

Amir is serious. He only knew it as he said the words aloud. "Skive off today?" he asks Mani, pretending he doesn't hear the note of pleading in his own voice. "I could really use a drink."

They end up going back to his. They take the bullet train in silence—it's mostly empty at this odd hour of the morning, but the tunnel-rush of wind makes holding a conversation difficult. The ride is only five minutes, but it's long enough to put Amir on edge. He stares down at his interlaced fingers, bracketed by his knees. There's an empty seat between him and Mani, because there was space to spread out, and why would they not? After all, these days, it's not like they're—well. It's like they're barely friends.

Mani has never been to Amir's apartment. He realizes this as he keys into the front door; they've tried, a few times, vague agreements about dinner that fell through at the last moment, meetings that wound up getting moved to workspaces with excuses of better bullet access. It should make him nervous, he thinks. He should be worrying about the fact that none of his coffee mugs match, or whether he left toothpaste flecks on the bathroom mirror that morning, but he isn't nervous. Mani knows all the worst parts of him already.

The Bekaa Valley Merlot is still at the back of the cupboard, because Amir's life is a joke. He uncorks it, pours them both generous glasses, and settles himself next to her at the small kitchen table. "There's a research institute in Nantes," he says. "They want to fund a Crowdgrow roll-out."

Mani looks stunned, just for a second, then raises her wineglass. "This is now a toast," she says. "To the long over-due recognition of my brilliant friend Amir Tarabi."

Amir tilts his glass toward hers. "Thing is," he says, "I'd have to start basically immediately. A few weeks. I wouldn't be here to close out Wet City. I wouldn't be able to make the launch festival."

" . . . oh," says Mani. She lowers her glass. "Damn."

"Right." Amir lowers his glass, too. He's not quite sure how to look at Mani, so he focuses on the wineglass, turning it in careful circles, watching the light refract. "I mean, it's not the end of the world," he says. "I'll need to pass some stuff off sort of hastily, but let's be honest, I'm no longer really essential personnel. And I don't care about the festival. It's just . . . "

Amir stops, looks up. He doesn't know how to read Mani's expression. Complicated, sad. A little like how she looks when she's working her way through a thorny problem. She reaches forward, finding his fingers with her own, carefully unlacing them from the stem of the wineglass. She holds his hand there in the warm cradle of her palms, running her thumb in a discovering sort of way across the line below his knuckles, as if she were going to read his fortune.

"It would have been nice," says Mani, "to have had more time."

"Mani," says Amir, helplessly. She looks up, looks at him. He feels on display, as if she's taking inventory of him, all the things that are different, all the things that are the same. He swallows. "I want—" he says.

Mani reaches up, running her fingertips through the scruff of his beard, bracing her thumb against his cheekbone. "Come here," she says. He goes, letting her guide him forward until she finds his mouth with hers, and kisses him.

His mind goes blank. He's a teenager again, unsure what to do with his hands. He loves her so much he thinks he might fly into a million separate parts.

She undresses him first, won't let him help, won't let him touch, torturous slowness as she undoes every button, every hook. She runs her fingertips over all the planes and angles of him, pressing teasing thumbs into the hollows by his hipbones, and kisses him until he feels drunk with it. Then she lets him do the same to her, and she takes his hands and shows him where to touch, and he thinks this might be the most beautiful thing he's ever done.

Afterwards, they lie tangled together, exhausted, belly-to-flank, Amir's cheek pressed against the top of Mani's head. The warm reality of her, the slow swell-and-recede of her body against his, is almost too much to stand.

"I'm going to miss you," Amir says. "I'm going to miss you so much. It wasn't enough time."

He feels her pause, then twist to look at him. "I shouldn't have said that, earlier," she says, very serious. "We can't think that way. We have to say to ourselves, this was right. This was exactly enough."

Amir shuts his eyes, tips his head forward to rest against hers, and tries to believe it.

He keeps his eyes closed until they both fall asleep.

5: The Beam Comes On, Illuminating Us All

Amir arrives in France just after dawn on a foggy fall day. His out-breaths add frills of fog to Nantes' thick cloak of it. He keeps his Impulse off after landing. Sounds muffled, skin damp, his first impression of his new home is of being underwater.

He explores the city on foot, stopping for croissants then brioches then tartines. At sunset, he sits on the lawn of the Château des Ducs de Bretagne and tosses a bag of soy chips to two mallards and their ducklings paddling in the castle's moat. Impulse would help him form a mental map, but he knows if he turns it on he's going to look for a message from Mani; if there's none he's going to be heartsick, if there is one he's going to be heartsick.

Three things cycle through Amir's mind: first, how to make the most of this opportunity; second, how desperately he needs to recenter himself in personal growth practice; third, the problem he's had for most of his life, which is that he can't stop thinking about Mani.

Amir wakes up with the sun on his first morning in his Nantes apartment and he takes creaking steps that raise dust motes along the wood-grain floorboards. At the window he turns Impulse on and his heart rattles the split-second before his unreads appear.

Nothing from Mani.

Amir starts to compose a message. "Hi! Nantes is beautiful. There's a duckling in the castle moat who has learned to swim alongside—" then he closes his eyes, hard, and deletes. When he opens them the weathervane across from his window has flipped 180 degrees and the sun is a blur of honey.

The Crowdgrow pilot takes place along two residential streets in Nantes-2, just north of the Gare de Nantes. Amir hand-delivers cuttings of ecoboosted crawler vine to each of the experiment's participants.

"Je vous attends toute la matinée," says one girl when Amir puts the little red planter pot in her hands. Her tight cornrows have been braided into an orchid-shaped bun on top of her head. She takes him round to the back garden, shows him the sheltered hole in the soil she's dug. There is so much *care* in her actions that Amir's belief in—dedication to—Crowdgrow redoubles just like that.

"Mes mamans disent que le ciel sera plein d'oiseaux," she says.

"Yes," Amir replies through Impulse. "As many birds as the sky can handle."

Nantes is on a clean air travel vector with Beirut, so Joud comes to visit the week before Amir presents the results of the pilot to a delegation from the Nantes municipal authority. They go to Nantes shipyard island, to the mech-AI safari park. They feed the giant hydraulic elephants from a tray of silicon peanuts and the elephants regurgitate silicon caricatures of Amir and Joud. Joud's is great: an impossibly vertical cone of hair, small ears rendered as notches. Amir's own caricature makes him feel every day as old as his thirty-two years, and older.

He wraps their portraits up and tucks them in his bag, presses Joud close. Arm in arm, they survey nearby menus on Impulse until Amir finds one that does a much-lauded synth-protein steak with cassava fries. They wash it down with crisp, sweet Breton cider.

"To new avenues," Joud says.

"To the companions who walk our lives with us," Amir says. The words are from a passage Mani once clipped from a poem. He clinks the neck of his bottle against Joud's.

The first results come back from Crowdgrow in Nantes-2. The air quality in that sector has improved a modest part per billion, but what's really encouraging is that all the crawler vines have survived. Many have gained a meter or more in length. The pilot expands to a citywide project, Adah's grant money matched by government funds.

Amir comes home late one evening from overseeing a plant-in at a primary school, a little dazed from hours of sun and excitable schoolchildren, but in good spirits. He's got dirt all over, ground into the new callouses on his palms and spilling from the hems of his trousers. The soil here is still toxic, and he should probably wash it off before doing anything else, but his diminutive wrought-iron balcony gets an excellent view of the sunset, and he can't help but peel off his shoes and socks and sit down at the wooden folding table to watch it. The last flash of sunlight is winking out on the windows of the Cathédrale Saint-Pierre et Saint-Paul when his Impulse pings with a call from Mani.

He answers without thinking—or, he answers before he can let himself think about it. "Mani?" he says, a question, like it could be anyone else.

"Hi," says definitely-Mani. "Are you—"

"Free," says Amir, straightening a little, though she hasn't initiated holo. "I mean, I just got home from work. I was just—" He stumbles. *Watching the sunset* feels too corny. "Relaxing," he finishes.

"Good," says Mani. "I saw on the Beirut Grid announcement stream that your project won that funding extension from the city. Wanted to say congratulations. So, well." She laughs a little. "Congratulations."

Amir sinks back into his chair. "Thanks," he says. "You too. I watched your speech at the launch ceremony. It was really beautiful."

"Thank you," says Mani. "I read your message to the team."

He'd figured she had, even when she didn't respond. He's not sure what to say to this.

"You should have been there," Mani says.

On the morning of the Wet City launch festival in Beirut, they'd got the first full bloom on a crawler vine in Nantes-2, a pale blue flower veined with green, nearly the size of Amir's head. The stem wasn't robust yet; the smallest breeze set the blossom trembling, like at any moment it might come free and drop to the earth. Amir had spent most of the morning crouched in the dewy garden, waiting to see if it would last. "That's kind of you," says Amir, "but you were fine without me."

The connection goes so silent Amir has to check Impulse for the activity blip.

"It's been harder," says Mani, "than I thought it would be."

Amir closes his eyes. He wants to say: I would come back if you asked me to. He wants to say: I wouldn't have left in the first place. Instead he says, "Mani."

"I love you," says Mani. "Even if we never quite figure out what that should look like. You know that, right?"

The breeze is sharpening with night, carrying scents of yeast and toffee from the bakery on street level. The latticework of the metal balcony presses geometry into the soles of Amir's feet. He can hear the soft hush of Mani's breath, in and out.

"Yes," says Amir. "I know."

Over the next seven years Nantes becomes a garden city. Every green space is verdant with ecoboosted flora from Amir's program; parks and groves are remade from concrete lots and musky alleys. The skies, as one little girl had once hoped, are full of birds.

Amir spends one of those years working with his team on tweaks to the Crowdgrow flora to ensure the boosted species are hospitable to native ones, and that summer there are small populations of roe deer, and bushes of garden aster, and swallows, and a sighting of a pair of endangered partridges on the steps of the Théâtre Graslin.

Mani stays in Beirut after Wet City launches, takes up a just-formed position as Beirut's Minister for Enrichment. Amir pieces together through her understatements and Impulse research that this means she oversees almost every program in Beirut that impacts on quality of life standards for natural lighting in modular housing, breeding programs for Mediterranean loggerhead turtles, the national poetry curriculum. He's immensely proud and touched.

Amir thinks about surprising Mani in Beirut for her thirty-sixth birthday; he's been back home twice while Mani was away on diplomatic visits, just bad luck. He asks circumspect questions to make sure she'll be in town, buys a ticket. The day before the flight he gets scary news: one of the Crowdgrow fern populations has been proliferating invasively, killing off a native garden. Amir gets on a bullet to Nantes-11 and he's so nervous about the clean-up operation he doesn't see the inside of his apartment for three days.

They control the fern; he misses his chance to visit Mani.

Time goes so quickly in those years, but he spends more evenings sitting on his balcony watching the sunset than not.

It's Adah who brings Amir the news personally: they've received an application to start a Crowdgrow program in Beirut.

It'll be the seventeenth spin-off of the original Nantes pilot—the first three Amir went to oversee himself, spending months in Bruges, Liverpool, Alexandria. After that, they'd developed a formula, easy for new cities to follow with only a few weeks' oversight from Amir's staff.

"It's below your pay grade," says Adah. "But I thought you might want to take this one on yourself. Chance to catch up with old friends. But we'll send someone else if you're too busy."

Amir is definitely too busy. "Don't send anyone else," he says. "I'd love to go."

Amir calls Mani that afternoon as he's walking home from work, feeling like something in him is unfurling in the late autumn sun. "I hear someone in Beirut ordered some mutant daisies," he says the moment she picks up.

"Smug," Mani says. "I was so pleased when the proposal came through."

"Me too. And, um. Adah asked if I wanted to come do the kickoff myself."

There's a pause. "What did you say?"

Amir huffs. "I said yes, obviously! What do you think?" He scruffs his knuckles over the stubble on his jawline, tries to keep his voice casual.

"I'll clear my calendar," Mani says.

Amir's Impulse pings with an unread as his plane begins to descend into Beirut. Joud. *Meet at the rock wharf by al-Raouché, bring a warm coat.*

It's five a.m. and Amir has had no sleep. He's really getting too old for no sleep, but the trembly adrenaline of night flights and home is a jolt in his chest, so he goes, his luggage tracking him at a polite distance.

The wind is insistent and briny. Amir seals his coat to his chin. There's a huge crowd at the wharf, and food kiosks, banners, a bunch of institutional logos he doesn't recognize, and one he does—Beirut Grid's.

Joud finds him where he's paused at a corniche railing trying to work out the reason for the commotion. He hasn't seen Joud in two years, not since Joud moved into a rundown mountain house in Ehden with three partners and their five little ones to begin hand-renovating the house to ecopositive standards.

They look great. Sun-hardened, their hair a wiry nest of salt and pepper, clipped a little closer than Amir remembers.

"There's a team from Beirut Grid here," Joud says when they hug. "And a couple of my kids. I want you to meet them. Leave the luggage, come."

Joud leads Amir into the wharf and onto the rocks beyond, where adults and children are queued up to use what look like fishing poles. There's a din of excitement and an occasional whoop of triumph.

Amir is stunned. "Are they *fishing*?"

Joud laughs, just as three little humans run into their arms shouting, "We fed one!"

"Show Amir," Joud says, and a kid with the same shy grin as their parent holds out a glossy pellet cradled in their palm.

"Vitamin feed to correct an imbalance in the ecosystem," says Joud. "It's civic engagement, a bit of publicity. There's a water-soluble version they'll pump in after."

"Joud?" asks the smallest child. "Are they going to come live with us?" They glance at Amir. "We have enough water for them to do a mineral soak once a week too."

"He's welcome to come live with us," Joud says, and Amir forces himself not to look away from the softness on Joud's face.

"Amir Tarabi! Of all the fish-feeding parties in all the towns . . . " says someone behind him. He turns around to see Mesilla carrying a pail, and behind her Hanne and Caveg.

"This is crazy," Amir says, and gathers them into a hug. "I just got off the plane from France. How . . . "

"Maybe not totally a coincidence." Joud winks at him. "I thought Mani would be here too, but her assistant told me she's working a short day today, had to wrap things up at the ministry."

Hanne cracks a joke about Amir still overthinking everything, except now in French, and it's one of those moments the younger Amir wouldn't have believed in: like the universe has turned its spotlight on him, for a fleeting instant, and instructed him to rest.

Eventually, the trajectory of the future will look like this: some years, Amir in Beirut, guest lecturing at the Pan-Humanist Polytechnic, consulting on the new ecoboosted installation in Zahleh, taking a sabbatical to work on a collection of essays about crowdsourcing civic change. Some of those years, Mani in Beirut too, but others, Mani in the Arctic, Mani back in Mogadishu, Mani on the Gulf Coast. Once, eighteen glorious months both in Beirut, a routine of dinner parties at Mani's girlfriend's loft apartment, and stargazing every third weekend during Beirut's Dark Skies nights: picnic blankets and wine, Amir's head in Mani's lap, Mani's fingers in his hair. Once, ten long years where the vagaries of circumstance mean they don't manage to see each other at all.

Eventually, all the days in a human life, whether or not they feel like enough.

For now, all the hard, gut-ache hope and all the pragmatics and all the inexorable decades coalesce like this: Amir steps out of a Beirut hotel two streets up from his old al-Manara apartment holding a potted Crowdgrow cutting, and points himself toward Stella Kadri Square.

Mani messages him just as he spots the showcase Wet City wings fanning out in the distance, describing the perimeter of the brand new square. Their bugs-in-amber make them into a museum of petrified art. He saw hundreds of the wings from the air and he'd seen the beachfront ones from a distance on his brief visits home, but now they *strike* him. It's like walking toward the foot of a mountain, that same organic rightness of approaching and finding the world continuing up and out beneath his feet.

Mani sends him the geo for a bench she's found. He wants to play that old game of how long has it been, but he draws every minute of personal growth he's ever done to ground himself—he notes the flinty musk of impending rain, the drawn out ping of the bullet slicing across the city, the tickle in his throat from the boosted pollen of the Crowdgrow cutting. His heart, beating in his neck.

Amir spots the bench from a distance. Mani is a blue-coated speck on one side of it. He's shy, suddenly, walking into a casual get-together with Beirut's Minister for Enrichment, walking across the grandeur of a public space he knows she conceived and oversaw to completion, a tribute to the world Mani's rallied for and railed against so passionately her whole life. Then Mani messages him a biofeedback wave, and Amir viscerally feels her excitement hum in his brain, and he's not shy anymore. He wants to be near enough to touch her so badly he almost breaks into a run.

But doesn't. He gets close enough for her to hear him and shouts "Mani!" Her peacoat is the shade of the ocean, collar drawn up. Her face is open and happy. Amir can't believe she could possibly wear that expression for him.

"You look like you're having a pretty good day," he laughs.

She shakes her head, gets up, closes the distance and hugs him, her cheek is right over the brutal hammering of his heart. Amir stands as still as he can, clutching the

Crowdgrow pot against Mani's back, waiting for the moment she breaks the embrace, kind of hoping that will be never.

"I brought you a cutting," Amir says.

"Welcome home," Mani mumbles. Her voice vibrates in his chest.

"To us both," he says.

She turns her face up to his and puts fingers on his jaw and kisses him and doesn't stop, and Amir must really be in a kinder world because it starts to rain, raindrops that splatter open, big and clean and warm.

The Standard of Ur

by Hassan Abdulrazzak

Hassan Abdulrazzak is of Iraqi origin, born in Prague and living in London. His plays include Baghdad Wedding *(Soho Theatre, 2007, Belvoir St Theatre, 2009, Akvarious, 2010),* The Prophet *(Gate theatre, 2012),* Love, Bombs and Apples *(Arcola Theatre, 2016 and UK tour. Golden Thread, San Francisco, 2018) and* And Here I Am *(Arcola Theatre, 2017 and UK and Middle East tour). His contribution to anthologies include* Iraq+100: Stories from a century after the invasion *(Comma Press, 2016),* A Country of Refuge *(Unbound, 2016),* Don't Panic, I'm Islamic *(Saqi Books, 2017) and* A Country to Call Home *(Unbound, 2018). He is the recipient of George Devine, Meyer-Whitworth and Pearson theatre awards as well as the Arab British Centre Award for Culture.*

12.02.2103

18:37

My granddad used to tell me that there were only two things he was afraid of: sharks and somehow finding himself in Iraq. I am on my way to, of all places, Baghdad. For a long time Iraq was synonymous with violence and mayhem. Grandad didn't live to see the change.

The British Museum, my employer, has sent me on this assignment. The trip is funded by the Iraqi ministry of energy, which is a good thing considering the state of the British economy. I can't screw it up. I fought so hard to get this job. I was the first in my family to attain a full time job or FTJ as they are more commonly known. My father said—with teary pride—that it was only appropriate I got a FTJ at the British Museum because FTJs seem like relics of the past.

A part of me is afraid to make the trip. My name is Adam. I come from Hounslow. I'm 28. I have blond hair and can only manage rudimentary Arabic. In previous times I would have been a perfect target for kidnapping. I keep assuring myself that things are different now in Iraq, that I will be all right, but I can't help the slight anxiety running like a current along my spine.

23:06

Shit, check out this hotel! It's mega plush. I've stayed in Paris Hiltons before but this one is special. I guess the solar energy boom has been good to Iraq. At the airport I was met by two employees from the ministry of culture. A guy called Othman, mid-30s, burly, thick moustache, like that of the famous Iraqi dictator. He is going to be in charge of my security. He was accompanied by a woman, Ishtar. Early 20s, short curly hair, big oval eyes, thin and pointed nose, altogether very pretty. She seems polite, matter of fact, and pliable. Ishtar has a PhD in Near Eastern studies and is going to be my facilitator for the duration of the stay.

A note about my language skills. At University I learnt Sumerian and Akkadian. That's how I landed the museum job. My Arabic is touch and go.

The foreign office advised that I don't risk direct exposure to the elements, even at night when the temperature is more bearable. Drought is an even bigger problem here than heat. My bosses assured me that I would be supplied with water throughout the trip.

Othman and Ishtar took me to the car bay area inside the airport. We drove through one gate, which instantly locked. A second gate opened allowing us to leave the building. This double gate system is designed to minimise exposure.

In the ride from the airport to the hotel, Ishtar transferred an itinerary onto my tablet. It was mainly meetings with various officials from the ministries of culture and energy as well as a visit to the new museum in Ur. Her oval eyes widened when I told her this wouldn't do. I didn't come all this way to shake hands and take photos. I needed to see it.

"See what?"

"The first city."

"This wasn't part of the agreement."

"I have to see it. The temple."

"It's not open to visitors."

"If you don't take me there then the transfer will not even be considered."

Ishtar looked very irritated as she made a few calls. At the hotel, she told me that she would let me know in the morning if my request could be granted. I bid her goodnight and headed to my room.

On my bed, instead of the usual chocolates you get at hotel rooms elsewhere, there was a small bottle of mineral water.

13.02.2103

09:36

Ishtar showed up at breakfast. She told me that Othman would be picking us up in one hour and we would be heading to the first city, as I desired. I was astonished, as I had assumed she would have to battle through a hell of a lot of bureaucracy to make it happen.

"I spent all last night trying to arrange this trip. Most people I spoke to at the ministry were against it."

"Why?"

"Bad things happen in the first city."

"Bad things like what?"

"Just bad things."

"Just tell me what bad things," I insisted.

"It's ever since the Germans completed phase three of the temple excavation. People have been feeling a little strange."

"Did they unleash a virus?"

"No, I don't think it's anything that bad. Just follow my instructions and you'll be fine."

She got up.

"Where are you going?"

"I'll see you at the entrance in one hour."

I watched her walk away. I was hoping that Ishtar might be someone I could invite to a Q&A session at the exhibition I wanted to organise. It would lend the enterprise an air of authenticity to have an Iraqi present.

I went to my room and screen timed my father. We argued for several minutes. He was worried about me.

"I'll be fine, Dad."

"Your granddad would've been dead set against this trip."

"Granddad lived in different times."

"Iraq, until very recently, was a dangerous place."

"Twelve years is hardly recently."

"I find it weird, don't you?"

"What's weird?"

"Their solution for the violence. It's not right."

"It works. That's what matters," I said whilst updating my status on social media, showing off about the trip I was about to undertake.

"Watch yourself, son."

That was the longest conversation we'd had in a long while.

13:30

We've been on the road heading south now for two hours.

I am riding in the hotel shuttle with Ishtar and Othman. The driver is a man called Abu Jaafar, in his late 40s. He has a jovial manner and his tanned face beams as he speaks.

"Hello, Mr. Adam. Welcome... welcome. This is my Kasir van. How you say Kasir in English?"

Before Ishtar has a chance to speak, I jump in.

"Palace."

"Yes. It is palace. It has everything. Water, cold, food. It is like Green zone. You know Green zone?"

The Green zone is the old name given to Government City. It is fascinating to me that locals still use this century-old name for the site of government buildings rather than its official name. An old professor of antiquity once told me that in Iraq, all historical eras, including deep antiquity, course through the veins of modern Iraqis. I looked at Abu Jaafar's open, tanned face and imagined an old Sumerian builder constructing a city wall, out in the open, sweat beads gathering along his forehead like pearls.

"You smoke, Mr. Adam?"

"No, thanks."

"It's OK, you in Iraq. You can smoke. You no in West anymore."

"Really, it's very generous of you but no thanks."

Abu Jaafar picked up a small electric shisha, took a deep breath, and let out a puff of vapour. The van filled with the smell of apples. He laughed heartily.

"Smoke make me happy. I smoke, I love all people. East, West, Shimal, Janoub. Everybody. We have palace van, we have shisha, we have music, we have water, we have the beautiful Ishtar who is always on computer."

Ishtar looked up briefly at Abu Jaafar. I don't think she smiled. She buried her head in her tablet once again and continued typing what seemed like an essay length email. Is she reporting to her superiors about me?

"Keep your eye on the road," commanded Othman, brushing his thick moustache.

"Whatever you say, boss," replied Abu Jaafar.

Did I sense a slight animosity between Othman and Abu Jaafar? Perhaps that was all in my head. From their names and from my rudimentary knowledge of Iraq, I could tell that Othman was a Sunni and Abu Jaafar a Shia, but animosity between Sunni and Shia is a thing of the past now thanks to The Solution.

"Today is going to be a good day," declared Abu Jaafar as he pumped the gas pedal.

I saw several old buildings with boarded up shops. It's fascinating to think that as early as thirty years ago, there were shops facing the street and people walked on the pavement during the day. You could see people walking in heat suits, heading to the nearest shopping mall.

"So why are you interested in Uruk?" Ishtar asked.

"I'd like to organise an exhibition about the first city."

"Are you sure it is the 'first' city? We've discovered new cities in the south, some think they are bigger and older than Uruk."

"I've seen no publication to confirm that," I replied.

"I have friends who are working on this. Sumer was a much bigger civilisation than you realise."

Her voice was rising. I hadn't suspected that Ishtar had this passionate side to her.

"Your friends need to publish if that is the case."

Before she had a chance to reply, the car came to a sudden, jerky stop.

"Ibn el Khara [son of a shit]," shouted Abu Jaafar, momentarily losing his jovial nature. A man had run past him. We all stared at the man through the thick windows. He was naked, his arms raised to the sky. He ran into the middle of the road and stared at the sun.

"Ya Allah!" cried Ishtar.

"He won't last a minute!" Othman shouted.

Abu Jaafar was blaring his horn, alerting other cars to the man's presence.

I was scrambling for my camera, cursing my luck. It had snagged on the latch of my leather bag. The naked man's arms seemed to rise higher and higher. Suddenly two policemen in heat suits ran towards the man with a reflective blanket. As they draped the blanket over the man, little strands of smoke swirled up in the air.

Cars behind us were beeping.

"Wait, don't move!" I shouted at Abu Jaafar as I kept pulling at the stuck camera. More cars joined the orchestra of beeping and eventually Abu Jaafar ignored me and drove on. My camera finally dislodged. I turned it on and tried to film but it was too late.

"Shit!"

"Why did you want to film that?"

"He looked like Jesus. It was magnificent."

Ishtar shook her head with disapproval and buried her head in the tablet. I realised that my fevered desire to capture the man burning in the sun on camera might have come across as somewhat callous so I asked: "Was the man committing suicide?"

Othman looked alarmed. I think he feared that what happened could influence my evaluation negatively. "It's nothing, Mr. Adam. Nothing." He then leaned forward and asked me if I had managed to film anything.

"Censorship, really? How quaint," I said.

"It's not censorship exactly, Mr. Adam. It's just … this is a sensitive time for Iraq," said Othman, brushing his moustache with his fingers. "We are transitioning to full stability."

"That man didn't look stable."

"It happens," said Ishtar. "Some people have the urge to breathe real air."

"Is that what he was doing?" I asked.

She shrugged. "There is a movement happening. People demanding climate reform. They are asking for the right to be in the open air again."

"Did you ever experience the open air?"

She shook her head. At that moment I wanted to put my arms around her. To give her a consolatory hug. It is still possible to breathe real air in England. I am privileged.

"I am sorry that you ..."

"Don't be," she snapped and buried her head in her tablet again, typing away furiously. She doesn't make it easy to get close to her, that's for sure. She's certainly not as pliable as I first thought. This was a while ago, now everyone has dozed off. I am feeling sleepy, too. I'll stop typing.

15:45

It has taken another hour since my last journal entry to reach Uruk, the first city. I don't care if Ishtar is right and Uruk turns out not to be the first human city. I'll call it the first city in my exhibition. Sometimes with history you need a semi-myth to fire the public's imagination. At a time of crisis for cities around the world: over population, pollution, heat, floods, drought, old viruses resurrecting from the melted ice sheets, at such a time, there will be curiosity to cast our collective minds back to the first city, even if such a place never really existed. What is known about Uruk is that it was here that writing first emerged at around 3000 BC, give or take a thousand years depending on who you read. The city housed 10,000 people, some say as many as 50,000 people. Here the first system of writing was developed, but perhaps more importantly for our times, it was here that the first consumer product was invented: the disposable beveled-rim bowl, a kind of tin foil of its day, probably used for handing out food to workers. And here I was, finally, standing on the ground I had read and thought about so much.

In the van we had scrambled to put on our heat suits. Ishtar slipped into her suit quickly and elegantly like a child sliding down a water chute; Othman being a bear of a man, struggled into his; Abu Jaafar was already wearing the leg part of the suit. He wasn't meant to leave the van but curiosity got the better of him.

"I come to Uruk child. Five, six. With father. Allah yerhamah [God have mercy on his soul]. You could be outside in real air back then."

"Stay in the van, Abu Jaafar," commanded Othman.

"Ostath Othman, bes khames dagaek. [Mr Othman, just five minutes]." He then pleaded with him some more, I only caught fragments of the Arabic, but I think he was saying that he wanted to glance at the temple and then head back to the van.

"Is it dangerous?" I asked Othman.

"No, no, not dangerous. It's just he is the driver. He has no business getting out of the van."

"Leave him be," interjected Ishtar. "If he wants to see the temple, he can. It's his right as an Iraqi."

That put Othman in his place. Abu Jaafar's face beamed once again and he quickly finished putting the rest of his heat suit on.

When we came out of the van, I had a momentary panic that I hadn't sealed the suit properly and my skin was going to burn like that of the naked suicidal man we had seen earlier. But once we saw the remnants of the temple, I soon lost all my apprehension.

It was magnificent. This particular temple was only discovered about fifty years ago by a German team. The excavation was supposed to be done by Britain but the money for it couldn't be raised and the Germans stepped in like smug saviours.

Over the door of the temple was a huge statue of the goddess Inanna, holding the rod and ring of justice, both Mesopotamian symbols of divinity. I approached the main gate of the temple, but as I stepped closer I realised that it had been sealed with a wooden door. A combination lock was on the latch.

"Can we go in?"

"No," said Ishtar firmly.

"Why not? I want to see what's inside."

"The structure ... it's not stable." I could sense she was lying. I noticed beads of sweat on her forehead through the visor of the heat helmet she was wearing.

"Are you okay, Ishtar?"

"I'm perfectly fine," she lied again. "Have you seen enough? Shall we go?"

"We just got here," I said, taking out my 3D camera.

I stepped back and eyed the statue of Inanna once again. Her ample breasts, her exposed belly, her round hips, all spoke of femininity and fertility.

"It's for you, this temple," I joked. I don't think Ishtar could see that I was smiling.

"Excuse me?"

"It's for the goddess Ishtar, your namesake. That's why they built it."

"Actually, it's for the goddess Inanna."

"Well, Inanna was the precursor to Ishtar who is the precursor to Aphrodite who is the precursor to Venus."

"Oh please."

"What? It's true."

"Aphrodite and Venus are all about beauty and sexual power."

"Inanna and Ishtar had plenty of sexual power."

"Inanna was a goddess of war. You Europeans took our deities and turned them into wet dream fantasies."

"You say that like I was personally responsible."

"What are you doing here, Adam?" She was sweating profusely now.

"I want to document the site."

I began to record the site with the 3D camera. The footage would be fantastic for the exhibition.

"You are supposed to be here to evaluate whether we can get the Standard of Ur back."

"I know that. But I'm also fascinated by Uruk."

"This is not why the British Museum sent you. You shouldn't even be here. You should be in Ur, inspecting the new museum we've built."

"Uruk is what, fifty kilometres from Ur? All this will be a tourist trail once the museum opens."

"This is a personal project, isn't it? A way for you to get a leg up in the world. Typical European, climbing to the top on the back of Orientals."

I could see that the sweat was pouring down her face now.

"It's not like that. Look, I was thinking that you could be a guest speaker at my exhibition."

"I don't want to play the role of the native informant, thank you. And besides, I've seen London in VR."

"Virtual reality doesn't do it justice."

"It's nothing, a city in decline."

"That's not true."

She steamrolled me. "And your British Museum is not a museum, it's a thief's den done up like Disney."

"I think you and I got off on the wrong…"

"Do your job, Mr. Adam. Evaluate. And evaluate fairly. The Standard of Ur belongs to us and you know it."

She headed towards the van, leaving me guiltily clutching my 3D camera. I mapped the site as best I could. I noticed Abu Jaafar standing before the statue of Inanna, mesmerised. He too was sweating profusely. Strange that I felt just fine inside my heat suit. Abu Jaafar seemed transfixed by the statue, as if he was communicating telepathically with Inanna.

"Abu Jaafar!" I cried to him so he would turn towards me and I could capture him fully on camera. But he didn't move. Then as if he had a delayed reaction, he snapped back to reality. "She is a beauty, no?" he said. I nodded. The cheerful smile returned to his face. He walked slowly back to the van, taking occasional glances at Inanna over his shoulder.

As I continued my mapping, I thought about the Standard of Ur. This is an object that has taken pride of place at the museum for the past four centuries. It is not physically impressive like the Assyrian winged human-headed lion, being nothing but a hollow box about eight, nine inches wide and some twenty inches long, yet it is a remarkable window into another world. The box is inlaid with a mosaic of shell, red limestone, and lapis lazuli and decorated with scenes of war and peace. On the peace side, you see in one panel the king enjoying a drink with his companions, attended by servants and entertained by a musician playing the lyre accompanied by a long-haired male singer. The details are so clear, you are transported to that royal scene, almost hearing the music. On the war side, in the lower panel you see the king's chariots running from left to right with increasing speed, like the frames of an old fashioned film. Underneath the rapidly moving chariots are the trampled naked enemies of the king, who lie bleeding. And right there on that small, seemingly insignificant box that dates to around 2500 BC lies the entire gamut of human civilisation.

The Standard was discovered by Sir Leonard Woolley in the late 1920s in the corner of a chamber, lying close to the shoulder of a man who may have held it on a pole, which is why Woolley called it a 'Standard.' Yet subsequent investigations have failed to confirm this assumption so the box has retained an air of mystery all these centuries. What was the purpose of it exactly? We can only guess.

I can understand Ishtar's desire to see the Standard housed in an Iraqi museum. Yet I have to make sure that this unique object will be properly looked after. The museum is facing hard times at the moment and the price the Iraqi ministry of energy is willing to pay for the Standard could ease our financial burdens. Exhibitions like the one I am planning could be better funded and the museum could become relevant once again as it was in previous centuries. Yet can we really part with such a priceless object? Is that the right thing to do?

When I was done, I went back in the van. "Don't take off your heat suits," announced Othman. "We'll soon be in Ur."

14.02.2103

03:15

So much has happened! I don't know if I'll have time to write it all down.

As we drove towards Ur, we could all sense that something wasn't right with Abu Jaafar. He was swearing at the cars that overtook him. He started to drive rather fast and didn't mind the potholes as he had done before. Every time the van went over a pothole, we all smacked our heads on the van's roof.

"What the hell is the matter with you, Abu Jaafar?" Othman said in Arabic (or something close to this).

Abu Jaafar just kept driving faster and faster and cursing under his breath.

Ishtar pleaded with him to slow down but to no avail. We were being thrown around as Abu Jaafar switched from one lane to the next.

"Slow down, you idiot, or I'll have you fired!" Othman said in Arabic. He may have used 'animal' instead of 'idiot.'

Suddenly Abu Jaafar started screaming in English at Othman: "Shut up, bastard! You shut up. You are dirty Sunni. You are shit. You shut up when I talk. You shut up."

He now turned around and began flashing Othman with a hand gesture (waggling the middle finger).

"Fuck you, dirty Sunni. Fuck you."

We were now in the wrong lane. A big truck was heading straight at us. Othman leapt across the vehicle, turned the wheel of the car and the van spun off the road, crashing through a metal barrier and tumbling down a sandy hill.

I couldn't tell where I was or which way up we were. We tumbled for what seemed like infinity. Then eventually the van came to a halt on its side. I must have passed out for a good ten minutes. When I awoke I was totally disoriented. I found that I was alone in the van. I undid the safety belt and landed with a thud on the side of the van. I then crawled through the shattered windshield. When I emerged from the van, there were feathers everywhere, and a horrid noise that sounded like screaming. Up on the hard shoulder of the motorway I could see the truck had come to a halt and its back door had sprung open. There were chickens everywhere, walking around, cooking slowly in the sun, squawking like the insane. I looked towards the desert away from the motorway and I could see my companions were walking, zombie-like towards the horizon. Amongst the chicken squawking, I could hear another sound. Human screaming. Instinctively I pulled a heat blanket out of the van and ran towards my companions. Please God, let her be alright. Why was I so worried about a woman who clearly detested me?

I ran on unsteady legs. Ahead I could see Ishtar walking like a shell-shocked soldier on a battlefield.

"Ishtar, wait!"

I grabbed her by the shoulder and turned her so she would face me. Her heat suit had been ripped at the chest so that her naked left breast was jutting through. My heart was thumping in my chest. She must be burning. But then I looked again at her breast and it seemed unharmed. How could that be? I didn't know what to do. I hesitated to touch her. Yet I knew that I had to act quickly so I cupped her breast and shoved it back through the torn suit then covered her with the heat blanket.

"Ishtar!" I tried to catch her gaze. Her eyes couldn't focus at first but then suddenly she looked at me. I felt as if I were staring into a stranger's eyes. I then heard a horrible scream coming from up ahead. I made sure the blanket was secure on Ishtar's body before running towards Othman and Abu Jaffar. When I arrived I saw Othman had mounted a supine Abu Jaafar and was smashing his skull repeatedly with a rock.

"Othman, stop!"

Othman raised the rock and brought it down sending bits of skull and brains flying everywhere like a mince machine gone haywire.

"Stop it, Othman!!"

This time he did stop. He found something in the mashed head of Abu Jaafar that he was looking for. He held it up against the sun. It was a computer chip.

He stood, pocketed the chip, and headed to the highway. Ishtar and I followed him. The truck driver was on the hard shoulder, wearing a cheap heat suit and looking panicked. Othman told him that he was from the ministry of culture, which made the man eye him suspiciously. There was nothing cultured about how we looked. Othman borrowed the man's tablet and made a call.

We were put up in a small hotel in Ur. It was adequate but hardly the Paris Hilton. A doctor was sent to examine us. Nothing was broken. We did not need hospital admission, just some alcohol to clean the few scratches on our bodies and a plaster or two. It took a while to check us in. I asked Ishtar if she was all right, if she could be on her own.

"I just need a hot shower," she said softly. The clerk explained that there was enough water in the tank for all of us to shower but that the hotel had run out of bottled drinking water. "There must be some shops around selling water," I said. He shook his head. "There is no water in the entire town."

I collapsed on the bed of my room. I was so exhausted. All I wanted to do was fall asleep. I then heard a knock on the door. It was Othman. He entered, sat on a chair by the small breakfast table, and lit a cigarette.

"I am so sorry about Abu Jaafar," he said.

"What happened? Why did he go berserk?"

"I don't know. I will have the chip in his head analysed."

"Are you telling me that The Solution doesn't work?"

"It works. It works very well. You have to believe me but ..."

"What?"

"I've heard that some people who visit the Inanna temple, well it does something to them."

"If that's the case, why did you agree to us going there?"

"Nothing this bad has happened before. People complained of headaches, things like that. Maybe there is something in the temple ground interfering with the chips. The Germans stopped the dig. That's why the temple door was

71

boarded up. Maybe the more they excavate, the worse things get. I don't know, I'm speculating."

"Did you have to kill him?"

"We can't take a chance. We can't go back to how it was. The violence." Othman took out a brown bottle from his pocket.

"I got you this."

I took the bottle, opened it, and sniffed.

"Whisky?"

"Yes, locally made. Don't worry. It's good. It's the closest thing to water I could get you."

"Do you want some?"

Othman shook his head. "I don't drink. I got it for you." He got up.

"Is there any way I can persuade you not to mention what happened today in your report to the British Museum?"

I raised my hand, indicating that I didn't want to have this conversation.

"I will leave you with this," he said, putting a flick knife on the table. On the handle of the knife was a map of Iraq.

"What's this for?"

"It's just a precaution, in case more people turn the way Abu Jaafar did. I doubt you will need it."

I closed the door behind Othman and went back to the bed. I lay across it without taking off my clothes. I began to think about The Solution.

After the 2003 invasion of Iraq by the USA, Britain, and their allies a century ago, the country descended into chaos. Sectarian warfare, terrorism, and chronic corruption were endemic. I'm not an expert on the period. My field is deep antiquity. However, I know that it is a matter of intense debate amongst historians who study the post-invasion period whether the chaos unleashed on Iraq was a deliberate policy by the invaders or a series of unintended consequences.

The chaos continued in one form or another for the best part of the past century. There were periods of stability, certainly, but not sustained stability. Violence was always around the corner. A bold method had to be tried.

A group of Iraqi computer scientists and neurobiologists carried out a small-scale experiment in Mosul. They implanted computer chips in the brains of the inhabitants of segregated neighbourhoods. The chip dampened any sectarian bad feelings that the neighbours had for one another. The experiment was a resounding success and it was debated in parliament whether a nationwide rollout of the chip was in order. This happened during a period of intense violence, and as a result, the motion was passed.

Opponents of The Solution argued that sectarian antagonisms were not a natural or inevitable feature of Iraqi society. Communal antagonism before the 2003 invasion was minimal, they said. The flames of sectarian violence were fanned by the USA and her Gulf allies on the one hand, and Iran and her cohort on the other. Supporters of The Solution said that this explanation, whilst true, did not solve the problem on the ground. Something radical had to be tried to bring long-lasting stability and The Solution was the best option. A referendum was carried out and the supporters of The Solution won by a slim majority.

The chip was shot up the nose of the subject, its robotic part cutting through the blood brain barrier. The chip took control of synapses critical for manifesting hate. A fine balance had to be achieved. The subject couldn't be turned into a gushing mess incapable of retaining some reservation about others. What was needed was a removal of animosity to the outer group, sufficient to create a functioning society. The effect of The Solution wasn't immediately felt in a reduction of terrorist acts (it was hard to get to the terrorists anyway so most of them were not chipped) but in the changing wider societal values. People started to hire others for jobs based on merit rather than sectarian identity, bad mouthing members of a different sect or ethnicity behind closed doors lessened considerably, a general atmosphere of good will prevailed. All this eventually led to a sharp reduction in violence and lawlessness. The Solution worked. Until now.

I could tell that Othman was not looking forward to reporting to his superiors that the chip appeared to be malfunctioning for reasons unknown. The stability of Iraq over the past twelve years was already translating into a flourishing economy and increased tourism. All that was at stake now.

Still, I had a job to do. I wrote a first draft of the report on my tablet.

I was exhausted when I finished. I lay on the bed and soon a dream took over. I dreamt that a doctor reached with a fine tweezers through my ears and pulled out a Solution chip from my brain. I was amazed in the dream to have such a chip in my head. How did it get there? I felt elated after its removal, experiencing a tremendous surge of power and freedom. I was no longer Adam but Dumuzid, the husband of the goddess Inanna. I was flying in search of the goddess. Through the cloud I could see her ahead, her wings spread out, beating. I flew faster. I wanted to be with her but couldn't catch up to her. Suddenly she stopped, turned around. It was Ishtar. She let out the most piercing shriek.

The shriek turned into a buzzing sound. Someone was pressing the buzzer outside my room. I opened the door. It was Ishtar.

"Did I wake you?"

"I wasn't asleep," I lied.

"I couldn't sleep either."

"Come in."

She sat on the same chair Othman had sat on earlier. She took out a cigarette.

"Do you mind?"

I shook my head. She lit it and inhaled deeply. She was tapping her feet nervously against the table.

"There is no water in the hotel. I can't shower."

"But the man downstairs said ..."

"He lied."

"Are you thirsty?"

"A little. Why? Do you have some water?"

"Not exactly."

I put the homemade whisky on the table. I found two glasses and poured. I handed her a glass. She took it apprehensively. I tapped her glass with mine. She downed her glass in one go.

"Wow, take it easy."

"More."

I poured another measure of whisky for her. This time she drank it more slowly.

"That feels good," she said closing her eyes, savouring the taste. She then opened her eyes and said, "Have you written your report?"

"I wrote a first draft."

"Have you sent it?"

"No."

"Don't mention today. Today never happened."

"I cannot not mention today. I was sent here to assess if the Standard of Ur will be safe and how can I make such an assessment after what happened?"

"What happened was an anomaly. I've never seen anything like it. Even when Iraqis from one sect hate someone from another sect they never, ever express it in the open way Abu Jaafar did. I don't understand it."

"He lost all inhibition."

"You must omit it from your report."

"You know I can't do that, Ishtar."

"I was a little girl when the violence was still endemic in Iraq. Before The Solution. I remember what it was like. What happened today, a driver going nuts, that's nothing. Do you understand? That's nothing."

"You wouldn't be shaking if it were nothing. I can see it got to you."

"You mustn't put it in the report."

"Iraq is not ready for the Standard of Ur."

"And who are you to decide?"

"Keeping the Standard at the British Museum allows researchers from all over the world to examine it in a safe and stable environment, that includes Iraqi researchers."

"Give me a break."

"Will you stop with your anti-Britishness for a minute, Ishtar, and think about what I am saying?"

"I have one word for you. Lady Layard."

"That's two words."

"Austen Henry Layard excavates in Nimrud and Nineveh. Finds unique cylinder seals. Instead of treating them with the respect they deserve, he turns them into a necklace for his bride, Enid, who shows it off to Queen Victoria. And you at the museum display that necklace with utter pride. You know what that's like? That's like me going to Britain, chipping at Stonehenge to decorate my parents' patio."

"What does this story prove? Do you know how many artefacts we have in our possession, how many we have restored, catalogued, made available to researchers? You can't hang your judgment on one story."

"The Standard belongs to Iraq."

"The Standard belongs to the world. Imagine it is brought to the Ur museum and some guy goes nuts like Abu Jaafar and shoots all the tourists coming to see it. And whilst he is at it, he shoots up the Standard itself. All this and much worse happened in Iraq in the last century. Incredible artefacts were lost to the world. Is that what you want?"

"You are treating us like children, deciding what's good for us. Do you know how insulting that is?"

"I'm sorry you feel that way."

"So you've made up your mind?"

"Ishtar, if you were in my shoes, if you were asked to report back to your employer, what would you do? Would you lie?"

We looked for a while at one another. Finally, she shook her head.

"There is only one thing left to do then," she said. "Drink."

We went through the bottle at a fair pace. The more we drank, the more relaxed we became. We talked about what attracted us to ancient antiquity, about the evolution of cuneiform writing, we quoted passages from the epic of Gilgamesh to one another. She put on music on her tablet and showed me a local dance. A lot of feet stamping was involved. She laughed every time I made a misstep. I was holding her hand when she lost her footing and bumped into me. Was that deliberate? We were very close now.

"I remember it," she whispered.

"Remember what?"

"You touching me out in the desert."

She took my hand and placed it on her breast. She then grabbed my head and kissed me fiercely. I was surprised at how things had escalated. One minute we are practically shouting at one another, the next kissing passionately. Of course, I realised that there had been a spark between us the first moment we met, hidden under layers of antagonism.

She pushed me onto the bed and straddled me. I wasn't used to losing control. I tried to turn her so that I would be on top, but she pinned me down. She was incredibly strong with a lean and muscular body. I put my hand on her breast again. I remembered how lost and vulnerable she was in the desert. Now she looked powerful and self-assured. Her Sumerian eyes were looking deep into my soul.

She took me inside her without breaking eye contact. We began to rock and I was trying hard not to come too early. She was riding me wildly. I felt like a horse that was being broken by its owner. Who is this woman? What does she want from me?

We made love three consecutive times. She had the energy of a she-devil. When she finally rolled off me and fell asleep, I felt immense relief mixed with regret. I wanted the love making to last forever and I wanted it to end. I feared and wanted her all at the same time.

I'm glad I got to the end of this entry before Ishtar woke up.

I'm going to recommend that the Standard is not returned. However, I will go ahead and organise the exhibition about the first city. I will convince my bosses to invite Ishtar to speak about it and the Inanna temple. Perhaps Ishtar will like London enough to stay longer. I like the idea of us becoming on and off lovers.

I'll get a few winks now.

23:59
Adam woke to the smell of coffee that Ishtar had brought to bed. To Adam she must have seemed like a woman transformed. Did he think that his cock had this magical effect

on her? Probably not. He had enough self-awareness to know that might not be the case. Yet he was clearly pleased with how things had turned out.

"You don't have to do that," he said with a smile as he took the coffee from her hands.

"The water is back. You can have a shower if you like."

"Okay."

There was something almost endearing about the way he said okay as if they had been a couple for a long time. She watched him go into the bathroom, heard him sing as he showered. He stood before her, drying himself. He looked at ease as if he had done this a thousand times.

"I need your help," she said with the expression of a powerless woman.

"Ishtar, look, I can't change the report."

"It's not that. I need help with something else. Will you come with me to the Inanna temple?"

"You want to go back?"

"There is something I want to show you."

She rented a car and drove with Adam along the same highway where they had the accident. She drove at a leisurely speed. They spoke about the possibility of her visiting London, of being a guest speaker at the museum. They traded anecdotes about being the geeky kids at school. They spoke of their first love.

"Today is Valentine's day," Adam said.

"I know that," Ishtar replied, not taking her eyes off the road. She enjoyed the silence that fell between them.

When they arrived at the temple, Ishtar led the way.

"Where are we going?"

"Inside."

"I thought you said we can't go inside."

"What I want to show you is inside."

Ishtar unlocked the combination lock to the wooden door. The temple was dark. Her eyes took a while to adjust to the darkness. Ishtar found a lamp, which she lit. There was a set of stairs descending below the temple. Ishtar led the way down the stairs, holding onto the lamp. It was a long flight of stairs and they were now deep under the earth. They finally reached a spacious chamber. Ishtar lit the lamps there and the room was soon bathed in a misty yellow light. Adam seemed mesmerised by the relief paintings all around, various depictions of the goddess Inanna. showing her magnificent wings, her owl-like talons gripping the backs of two lions. In the middle of the space was a stone platform.

"Is that what I think it is?"

"We think so. We're not sure."

"For humans?"

"Animals, most likely."

"Why do you need my help?"

"There is an inscription, very early, pre-cuneiform. We can't decipher it."

"Ah, you need the big bad Brit to do the job."

"Something like that."

"I was just kidding."

"I know."

Adam bent over the stone.

"Where is the inscription?"

"If you lie on your stomach over the stone, you'll see it better. It's at a very odd angle."

Adam did as he was instructed. By this point he had total trust in Ishtar.

Ishtar looked at his supine body. The one that, a few hours earlier, had given her some pleasure. She thought about stopping. She really did.

Ishtar plunged Othman's knife into Adam's back. The groan Adam let out was more in surprise than in pain. She turned him around. She wanted him to see her face as she plunged the knife with the map of Iraq in his heart.

"You took a trip in the desert and you never came back."

Plunge.

"But before that you sent the report. All is well. Iraq is ready for the Standard."

Plunge.

Adam spat out blood. It covered Ishtar's face and chest. She wiped it off.

"Ishtar!" he groaned.

"I am not Ishtar."

Plunge.

There was a flicker of recognition before the light went out entirely in Adam's eyes.

It wasn't hard for me to break into his tablet back at the hotel. Find the report and change the wording. This journal, which Adam must have thought was so secure, I hacked in six minutes. I copied it onto my tablet and deleted it from his. I decided to write this final entry, as I'm sure one day, far into the future, this will see the light of day. But for now they will never find Adam's body. He went into the desert, got lost, and died. It happens. Silly Brit.

I told him. He didn't listen. I told him Inanna was not Venus. She is much more than a sexual fantasy.

I am Inanna. And I live.

THE BAHRAIN UNDERGROUND BAZAAR

by Nadia Afifi

Nadia Afifi lives in the U.S., but grew up in the Kingdom of Bahrain in the Persian Gulf, where she watched the archipelago nation modernize and transform itself. She tells us that this science fiction story was inspired in part by imagining the home of her childhood in a hopeful light, with both its complicated past and a thriving future. Her first novel The Sentient *was released a couple months ago in September.*

Bahrain's Central Bazaar comes to life at night. Lights dance above the narrow passageways illuminating the stalls with their spices, sacks of lentils, ornate carpets, and trinkets. Other stalls hawk more modern fare, NeuroLync implants and legally ambiguous drones. The scent of cumin and charred meat fills my nostrils. My stomach twists in response. Chemo hasn't been kind to me.

Office workers spill out from nearby high-rises into the crowds. A few cast glances in my direction, confusion and sympathy playing across their faces. They see an old woman with stringy, thinning gray hair and a hunched back, probably lost and confused. The young always assume the elderly can't keep up with them, helpless against their new technology and shifting language. Never mind that I know their tricks better than they do, and I've been to wilder bazaars than this manufactured tourist trap. It used to be the Old Souk, a traditional market that dealt mostly in gold. But Bahrain, which once prided itself as being Dubai's responsible, less ostentatious younger cousin, has decided to keep up with its neighbours. Glitz and flash. Modernity and illusion.

I turn down another passageway, narrower than the last. A sign beckons me below — "The Bahrain Underground Bazaar." It even has a London Underground symbol around the words for effect, though we're far from its grey skies and rain. I quicken my pace down its dark steps. It's even darker below, with torch-like lamps lining its stone walls. Using stone surfaces — stone anything — in the desert is madness. The cost of keeping the place cool must be obscene. The Underground Bazaar tries hard, bless it, to be sinister and seedy, and it mostly succeeds. The clientele help matters. They're either gangs of teenage boys or lone older men with unsettling eyes, shuffling down damp corridors. Above them, signs point to different areas of the bazaar for different tastes — violence, phobias, sex, and death.

I'm here for death.

"Welcome back, grandma," the man behind the front counter greets me. A nice young man with a neatly trimmed beard. He dresses all in black, glowing tattoos snaking across his forearms, but he doesn't fool me. He goes home and watches romantic comedies when he isn't selling the morbid side of life to oddballs. This isn't a typical souk or bazaar where each vendor runs their own stall. The Underground Bazaar is centralized. You tell the person at the counter what virtual immersion experience you're looking for and they direct you to the right room. Or chamber, as they insist on calling them.

"I'm not a grandma yet," I say, placing my dinars on the front counter.

"Tell my son and his wife to spend less time chasing me around and get the ball rolling on those grandchildren." In truth, I don't care in the slightest whether my children reproduce. I won't be around to hold any grandchildren.

"What'll it be today?"

I've had time to think on the way, but I still pause. In the Underground Bazaar's virtual immersion chambers, I've experienced many anonymous souls' final moments. Through them, I've drowned, been strangled, shot in the mouth, and suffered a heart attack. And I do mean suffer — the heart attack was one of the worst. I try on deaths like T-shirts. Violent ones and peaceful passings. Murders, suicides, and accidents. All practice for the real thing.

The room tilts and my vision blurs momentarily. Dizzy, I press my hands, bruised from chemo drips, onto the counter to steady myself. The tumour wedged between my skull and brain likes to assert itself at random moments. A burst of vision trouble, spasms of pain or nausea. I imagine shrinking it down, but even that won't matter now. It's in my blood and bones. The only thing it's left me so far, ironically, is my mind. I'm still sharp enough to make my own decisions, and I've decided one thing — I'll die on my terms, before cancer takes that last bit of power from me.

"I don't think I've fallen to my death yet," I say, regaining my composure. "I'd like to fall from a high place today."

"Sure thing. Accident or suicide?"

Would they be that different? The jump, perhaps, but everyone must feel the same terror as the ground approaches.

"Let's do a suicide," I say. "Someone older, if you have it. Female. Someone like me," I add unnecessarily.

My helpful young man runs his tattooed fingers across his fancy computer, searching. I've given him a challenge. Most people my age never installed the NeuroLync that retains an imprint of a person's experiences — including their final moments. Not that the intent is to document one's demise, of course. People get the fingernail-sized devices implanted in their temples to do a variety of useful things — pay for groceries with a blink, send neural messages to others, even adjust the temperature in their houses with a mental command. Laziness. Soon, the young will have machines do their walking for them.

One side effect of NeuroLync's popularity was that its manufacturer acquired a treasure trove of data from the minds connected to its Cloud network. Can you guess what happened next? Even an old bird like me could have figured it out. All that data was repackaged and sold to the highest bidder. Companies seized what they could, eager to literally tap into consumer minds. There are other markets too though, driven by the desire to borrow another person's experiences. Knowing what it feels like to have a particular kind of sex. Knowing what it feels like to torture someone — or be tortured. Knowing what it means to die a certain way.

With that demand comes places like the Bahrain Underground Bazaar.

"I've got an interesting one for you," the man says, eyeing me with something close to caution. "A Bedouin woman. Want to know the specifics?"

"Surprise me," I say. "I'm not too old to appreciate some mystery."

My young man always walks with me to the sensory chamber, like an usher in a movie theater. It's easy for me to get knocked around amid the jostling crowds, and I admit that some of the other customers frighten me. You can always spot the ones here for violence, a sick thrill between work shifts. Their eyes have this dull sheen, as though the real world is something they endure until their next immersion.

"This is your room, grandma," the man says before spinning on his heels back to the front counter. I step inside.

The room is dark, like the rest of this place, with blue lights webbing its walls. I suspect they exist for ambience rather than utility. In the center of the room, a reclining chair sits underneath a large device that will descend over my tiny, cancer-addled head. On the back of it, a needle of some kind will jut out and enter my spinal cord, right where it meets the skull. It's painful, but only for a second, and then you're in someone else's head, seeing and hearing and sensing what they felt. What's a little pinprick against all of that?

I sit and lean back as the usual recording plays on the ceiling, promising me an experience I'll never forget. The machine descends over my head, drowning out my surroundings, and I feel the familiar vampire bite at my neck.

I'm in the desert. Another one. Unlike Bahrain, a small island with every square inch filled by concrete, this is an open space with clear skies and a mountainous horizon. I'm walking down a rocky, winding slope. Rose-colored cliffs surround me and rich brown dirt crunches underneath my feet. The bright sun warms my face and a primal, animal smell fills my nostrils. I'm leading a donkey down the path. It lets out a huff of air, more sure-footed than me.

I turn — "I" being the dead woman — at the sound of laughter. A child sits on the donkey, legs kicking. The donkey takes it in its stride, accustomed to excitable tourists, but I still speak in a husky, foreign voice, instructing the child to sit still. Others follow behind her — parents or other relations. They drink in the landscape's still beauty through their phones.

We round a corner and my foot slides near the cliff's edge. A straight drop to hard ground and rock. I look down, the bottom of the cliff both distant and oddly intimate. The air stills, catching my breath. Wild adrenaline runs through my body, my legs twitching. For a moment, I can't think clearly, my thoughts scrambled by an unnamed terror. Then a thought breaks through the clutter.

Jump. Jump. Jump.

The terror becomes an entity inside me, a metallic taste on my tongue and a clammy sweat on my skin. The outline of the cliff becomes sharper, a beckoning blade, while the sounds of voices around me grow distant, as though I'm underwater.

I try to pull away — me, Zahra, the woman from Bahrain who chooses to spend her remaining days experiencing terrible things. In some backwater of my brain, I remind myself that I'm not on a cliff and this happened long ago. But the smell of hot desert air invades my senses again, yanking me back with a jolt of fear. *Jump.*

A moment seizes me, and I know that I've reached the glinting edge of a decision, a point of no return. My foot slides forward and it is crossed. I tumble over the edge.

I'm falling. My stomach dips and my heart tightens, thundering against my ribs. My hands flail around for something to grab but when they only find air, I stop. I plummet with greater speed, wind whipping my scarf away. I don't scream. I'm beyond fear. There is only the ground beneath me and the space in between. A rock juts out from the surface and I know, with sudden peace, that that's where I'll land.

And then nothing. The world is dark and soundless. Free of pain, or of any feeling at all.

And then voices.

The darkness is softened by a strange awareness. I sense, rather than see, my surroundings. My own mangled body spread across a rock. Dry plants and a gravel path nearby. Muted screams from above. I know, somehow, that my companions are running down the path now, toward me. *Be careful*, I want to cry out. *Don't fall.* They want to help me. Don't they know I'm dead?

If I'm dead, why am I still here? I'm not in complete oblivion and I'm also not going toward a light. I'm sinking backward into something, a deep pool of nothing, but a feeling of warmth surrounds me, enveloping me like a blanket on a cold night. I have no body now, I'm a ball of light, floating toward a bigger light behind me. I know it's there without seeing it. It is bliss and beauty, peace and kindness, and all that remains is to join it.

A loud scream.

Reality flickers around me. Something releases in the back of my head and blue light creeps into my vision. The machine whirs above me, retracting to its place on the ceiling. I blink, a shaking hand at my throat. The scream was mine. Drawing a steady breath, I hold my hand before my eyes until I'm convinced it's real and mine. Coming out of an immersion is always disorienting but that was no ordinary immersion. Normally, the moment of death wakes me up, returning me to my own, disintegrating body. What happened?

I leave the chamber with a slight wobble in my knees. A tall man in a trench coat appears at my side, offering his arm, and I swat it away. I smile, oddly reassured by the brief exchange. This is the Underground Bazaar, full of the same weirdos and creeps. I'm still me. The death I experienced in the chamber begins to fade in my immediate senses, but I still don't look back.

"How was it?" The man at the front counter winks.

I manage a rasping noise.

"Pretty crazy, huh?" His grin widens. "We file that one under suicides, but it's not really a suicide. Not premeditated, anyway. She was a tour guide in Petra, with a husband, five children, and who-knows-how many grandchildren. She just jumped on impulse."

My mind spins with questions, but I seize on his last comment.

"I walked the Golden Gate bridge once, on a family trip," I say, my voice wavering. "I remember a strange moment where I felt the urge to jump over the edge, into the water, for no reason. It passed, and I heard that's not uncommon."

"They call it the death drive," the man says with a nod. His eyes dance with excitement and I understand at last why he works in this awful place. The thrill of the macabre. "The French have a fancy expression for it that means 'the call of the void.' It's really common to get to the edge of a high place and feel this sudden urge to jump. You don't have to be suicidal or anxious. It can happen to anyone."

"But why?" I ask. I suspect the man has studied this kind of thing and I'm right. He bounces on his heels and leans forward, his smile conspiratorial.

"Scientists think that it's the conscious brain reacting to our instinctive responses," he says. "You get to the edge of a cliff and you reflexively step back. But then your conscious mind steps in. Why did you step back? Maybe it's not because of the obvious danger, but because you wanted to jump. Now, a part of you is convinced you want to jump, even though you know what that means, and it scares you. Insane," he adds with undisguised glee.

"But most people don't," I say, recalling the terror of those moments at the cliff's edge.

"Most don't," he agrees. "That's what's interesting about this one. She actually went through with it. Why I thought you'd like it." His chest puffs up in a way that reminds me of my own son, Firaz, when he came home from school eager to show me some new art project. He stopped drawing when he reached college, I realize with sudden sadness.

"But what about…after she fell?" I ask. The fall was traumatic, as I knew it would be, but nothing from past

Nadia Afifi

immersions prepared me for the strange, sentient peace that followed the moment of impact.

"Oh, that," the young man says. "That happens sometimes. Maybe about ten percent of our death immersions. Kind of a near-death-experience thing. Consciousness slipping away. Those last brain signals firing."

"But it happened after I — after she fell," I protest. "She must have been completely dead. Does that ever happen?"

"I'm sure it does, but rarely," the young man says with a tone of gentle finality. He smiles at the next customer.

"Petra," I murmur. "I've always wanted to see Petra." And now I have, in a fashion.

Walking up the stairs, exhaustion floods my body. Some days are better than others, but I always save these visits for the days when I'm strongest. Leaning against the wall outside, I feel ready to collapse.

"Zahra? *Zahra!*"

My daughter-in-law pushes through the crowd. I consider shrinking back down the stairs, but her eyes fix on me with predatory focus. I'm in her sights. She swings her arms stiffly under her starched white blouse.

"We've been worried sick," Reema begins. Her eyes scan me from head to toe, searching for some hidden signs of mischief. For a moment, I feel like a teenager again, sneaking out at night.

"You really shouldn't," I say.

"How did you slip away this time? We didn't see you — "

"On the tracking app you installed on my phone?" I ask with a small smile. "I deleted it, along with the backup you placed on the Cloud." As I said before, I know more tricks than they realize. Thank goodness I don't have a NeuroLync. I'd never be alone. Of course, every time I sneak off after a medical appointment to walk to the bazaar, I'm battling time. They don't know when I've given them the slip, but when they return home from their tedious jobs to find the house empty, they know where I've gone.

Reema sighs. "You need to stop coming to this terrible place, Zahra. It's not good for your mind or soul. You don't need dark thoughts — you'll beat this by staying positive."

After accompanying me to my earliest appointments, Reema has mastered the art of motivational medical speak. She means well. It would be cliché for me to despise my daughter-in-law, but in truth, I respect her. She comes from a generation of Arab women expected to excel at every aspect of life, to prove she earned her hard-fought rights, and she's risen to the task. If only she'd let me carry on with the task of planning my death and getting out of her way.

On the way home, Reema calls my son to report my capture. Instead of speaking aloud, she sends him silent messages through her NeuroLync, shooting the occasional admonishing glance in my direction. I can imagine the conversation well enough.

At the bazaar again.

Ya Allah! The seedy part?

She was walking right out of it when I found her.

Is she okay?

Pleased enough with herself. What are we going to do with her?

Reema and Firaz work in skyscrapers along Bahrain's coastal business zone, serving companies that change names every few months when they merge into bigger conglomerates. To them, I'm another project to be managed, complete with a schedule and tasks. My deadline is unknown, but within three months, they'll likely be planning my funeral. It's not that they don't love me, or I them. The world has just conditioned them to express their love through worry and structure. I need neither.

I want control. I want purpose.

Firaz barely raises his head to acknowledge me when Reema and I walk through the kitchen door. He's cooking at ten o'clock at night, preparing a dinner after work. Reema collapses onto a chair, kicking off her heels before tearing into the bread bowl.

"I'm not hungry, but I'm tired," I say to no one in particular. "I'll go to bed now."

"Mama, when will this end?" Firaz asks in a tight voice.

I have an easy retort at the tip of my tongue. *Soon enough, when I'm dead.* But when he turns to face me, I hesitate under his sad, frustrated gaze. His red eyes are heavy with exhaustion. I, the woman who birthed and raised him, am now a disruption.

All at once, I deflate. My knees buckle.

"Mama!" Firaz abandons his pan and rushes toward me.

"I'm fine," I say. With a wave of my hand, I excuse myself. In the dark of my bedroom, images from the bazaar linger in the shadows. Echoes of blue lights dancing across the walls. I sink into my bed, reaching for the warmth I felt hours ago, through the dead woman's mind, but I only shiver. What happened in that immersion? The young man didn't fool me. I had experienced enough deaths in those dark chambers to recognize the remarkable. She jumped in defiance of instinct, but her final moments of existence were full of warmth and acceptance — a presence that lingered after death. What made her different?

The next morning, I take a long bath, letting Firaz and Reema go through their pre-work routine — elliptical machines, mindfulness, dressing, and breakfast, the house obeying their silent commands. After they leave, I take the bus downtown to the clinic.

I sit in a room of fake plants and fake smiles, chemicals warming my veins. Other women sit around me, forming a square with nothing but cheap blue carpet in the center. A nurse checks our IV drips and ensures our needles remain in place. My fellow cancer survivors — we're all survivors, the staff insist — wear scarves to hide balding heads. Young, old — cancer ages us all. Their brave smiles emphasize the worry lines and tired eyes.

Outside the window the city hums with its usual frenetic pulse. Elevated trains, dizzying lanes of cars, and transport drones all fight for space amid Bahrain's rush hour. Beyond it, the sea winks at me, sunlight glinting on its breaking waves. A world in constant motion, ready to leave me behind.

Coldness prickles my skin. Could I jump, like that woman jumped? It would be easy — rip the array of needles from my arm and rush across the room, and force the window open. I might have to smash the glass if they have security locks (a good strategy in a cancer ward). When the glass shatters and the screaming skyscraper winds whip at my hair, would I recoil or jump?

But I don't move. I cross my feet under my silk skirt and wet my lips. Perhaps I'm too fearful of causing a scene. Perhaps I'm not the jumping kind, but doubt gnaws at me with each passing second. Death is an unceasing fog around me, but despite my many trips to the bazaar, I can't bring myself to meet it yet.

Maybe you're not ready because you have unfinished business.

What could that be though? My child no longer needs me — if anything, I'm a burden. Bahrain has morphed into something beyond my wildest imagination. It's left me behind. I've lived plenty. What remains?

A rose city carved from rock. An ancient Nabataean site in Jordan, immortalized in photographs in glossy magazines and childhood stories. I always meant to go to Petra but had forgotten about that dream long ago, and in the Underground Bazaar, of all places, I'm reminded of what I've yet to do.

I close my eyes. The woman from yesterday's immersion tumbles through the air, beautiful cliffs and clear skies spinning around her. Is that why she was calm at the end? Did some part of her realize that she had lived the right life and was now dying in the right place?

The revelation hits me with such force that I have no room for uncertainty. I know what I must do, but I have to be smart about my next steps. The chemo session is nearly over. I smile sweetly at the nurse when she removes the last drip from my veins. My daughter-in-law will meet me downstairs, I reassure her. No, I don't need any help, thank you. This isn't my first rodeo. She laughs. People like their old women to have a little bite — it's acceptable once we're past a certain age. A small consolation prize for living so long.

In the reception room, I drop my phone behind a plant — Firaz and Reema are clever enough to find new ways to track me, so I discard their favorite weapon.

"Back again, Ms. Mansour? Looks like you were here yesterday." The man's eyes twinkle as he examines my record on his computer screen.

"Where did the woman live?" I ask. "The one from yesterday — the Bedouin woman. Does she have any surviving family?"

In truth, I know where she lived, but I need more. A family name, an address.

"Your guess is as good as mine," the man says. A different man, not my usual favorite. Tall and thin like a tree branch, with brooding eyes. I'm earlier than usual, so this one must take the early shift.

"Surely you have something." I inject a quaver in my voice. "Anyone with the NeuroLync leaves an archive of information behind." Unlike me, I don't add. When I go, I'll only leave bones.

"We don't keep those kinds of records here because we don't need them," he says. "People want to know what drowning feels like, not the person's entire life story."

"Well, this customer does."

"Can't help you."

This is ridiculous. When I was his age, if an older woman asked me a question, I would have done my best to answer. It was a period of great social upheaval, but we still respected the elderly.

I try another angle. "Are there any more paid immersion experiences tied to that record?" She's a woman, not a record, but I'm speaking in their language.

The man's eyes practically light up with dollar signs. "We've got the life highlight reel. Everybody has one. People like to see those before the death, sometimes."

Minutes later and I'm back in the immersion chamber, the helmet making its ominous descent over my head.

They call them "highlight reels," but these files are really the byproduct of a data scrubber going through a dead person's entire memory and recreating that "life flashing before your eyes" effect. Good moments and bad moments, significant events and those small, poignant memories that stick in your mind for unclear reasons. I remember an afternoon with Firaz in the kitchen, making pastries. Nothing special about it, but I can still see the way the sunlight hit the counter and smell the filo pastry when it came out of the oven.

The Bedouin woman's highlight reel is no different. There's a wedding under the stars, some funerals, and enough childbirths to make me wince in sympathy, but there are also mundane moments like my own. The smell of livestock on early mornings before the tourists begin spilling into the valley. Meat cooking over a low campfire. Memories that dance through the senses.

I leave the bazaar more restless than when I arrived. The woman's life was unremarkable. Good and bad in typical proportions. A part of me had expected a mystic connection to her surroundings, maybe a head injury that gave her strange conscious experiences that would explain her final moments. Instead, I found someone not unlike me, separated only by money and circumstances.

Through the humid air and dense crowds, Bahrain's only train station beckons. A bit ridiculous for an island, but it does connect the country to Saudi Arabia and the wider region via a causeway. I walk to the station, restlessness growing with each step. Perhaps this is my jump over the cliff. I'm moving toward a big decision, the pressure swelling as I reach the point of no return.

At the front booth, I buy a one-way ticket to Petra, Jordan, along the Hejaz Railway. Once I board the carriage, all my doubt and fear evaporate. This is what I need to do. A final adventure, a last trip in search of answers that no bazaar can give me.

The desert hills race by through the train window. It's hypnotic and before long, my mind stirs like a thick soup through old feelings. The terrain outside feels both alien and comforting, that sensation of coming home after a long trip. A return to something primal and ancient, a way of life that's been lost amid controlled air conditioning and busy streets. How can something feel strange and right at the same time?

The Hejaz Railway system was completed when I was a little girl, itself a revival and expansion of an old train line that was abandoned after World War One. The region re-asserting itself, flexing its power with a nod to its past. I've always hated planes, and you'll never get me on those hovering shuttles, so an old-fashioned train (albeit with a maglev upgrade) suits me just fine.

The terrain dulls as we speed north, as if the world is transitioning from computer animation to a soft oil painting. The mountains lose their edges and vegetation freckles the ground. Signs point us to ancient places. Aqaba. The Dead Sea. Petra.

The sun sets and I drift off to the engine's hum.

The next morning, the train pulls into Wadi Musa, the town that anchors Petra. I join the crowds spilling out into the station, the air cool and fresh compared to Bahrain. I reach into my pocket to check my phone for frantic messages, only to recall that I left it behind. Firaz and Reema must be searching for me by now. At this stage, they've likely contacted the police. Guilt tugs at the corners of my heart, but they'll never understand why this is important. Soon I'll be out of their way.

Ignoring the long row of inviting hotels, I follow the signs toward Petra. Enterprising locals hawk everything from sunscreen to camel rides. With my hunched back and slow gait, they trail me like cats around a bowl of fresh milk.

"*Teta,* a hat for your head!"

"Need a place to stay, lady?"

"A donkey ride, ma'am? It's low to the ground."

Why not? I'm in no condition to hike around ancient ruins. The donkey handler, a boy no older than eighteen, suppresses a smile when I pull out paper currency.

"How do most of your customers pay?" I ask as he helps me onto the beast.

"NeuroLync, ma'am. They send us a one-time wire."

"You all have NeuroLync?" I ask, amazed. Many of these locals still live as Bedouin, in simple huts without electricity or running water. "Yes, ma'am," he says, clicking his tongue to prompt the donkey forward. "We were some of the first in Jordan to get connected. Government project. Some refused, but most said yes."

Interesting. So the area's Bedouin and locals were early adopters of NeuroLync technology, an experiment to support the country's tourism. That explained how an elderly woman of my age had the implant long enough to record most of her adult life, now downloadable for cheap voyeurs. My chest flutters. *People like me.*

My guide leads the donkey and me down the hill into a narrow valley. Most tourists walk, but some take carriages, camels, and donkeys. An adventurous soul charges past us on horseback, kicking up red sand.

Along the surrounding cliff faces and hills, dark holes mark ancient dwellings carved into the rock. Following my gaze, my guide points to them.

"Old Nabataean abodes," he says, referring to the ancient people who made Petra home.

"Do people still live there?" I ask. My tone is light and curious.

"Not there," he says.

"So where do all of the guides and craftspeople live around here?" I follow up: "It makes sense to be close."

"Some in Wadi Musa, but mostly in other places around Petra. We camp near the Monastery and the hills above the Treasury."

I nod and let the silence settle between us, taking in the beauty around me. Suicide is a sensitive subject everywhere, but especially in the rural Arab world. I can't just ask about a woman who jumped off a cliff. But while I'm teasing away clues, I drink in the energy of my surroundings.

The warmth of the sun on my face, the sharp stillness of the air. The sense of building excitement as we descend into the narrow valley, shaded by looming mountains. We're getting close to the Treasury, the most famous structure in Petra. I can tell by the way the tourists pick up their pace, pulling out the old-fashioned handheld cameras popular with the young set. I smile with them. I'm on vacation, after all.

I've seen plenty of pictures of the iconic Treasury, knowing that no picture can do it justice. I turn out to be right. Ahead, the valley forms a narrow sliver through which a stunning carved building emerges. Its deep, dark entrance is flanked by pillars. Cut into the rock, its upper level features more pillars crowned with intricate patterns. Though ancient, it is ornate and well preserved. The surrounding throngs of tourists and souvenir peddlers can't detract from its beauty.

My guide helps me off the donkey so I can wander inside. It's what you'd expect from a building carved into the mountains — the interior is dark and gaping, with more arches and inlets where the Nabataeans conducted their business. For a second, my mind turns to Firaz and Reema, with their endless work. I look down, overwhelmed. People once flooded this building when it was a vibrant trade stop — people long gone. Everyone taking pictures around me will one day be gone as well — all of us, drops in humanity's ever-flowing river.

"Where next, ma'am?"

The winding road up to a high place, one you need a pack animal to reach. An easy place to fall — or jump.

"I'd like to see the Monastery."

On the way up the trail, I talk with my guide, who I learn is named Rami. He has the usual dreams of teenage boys — become a soccer player, make millions, and see the world. When I tell him where I live, his eyes widen and I'm peppered with questions about tall buildings and city lights. He talks of cities as though they're living organisms, and in a way, I suppose they are. Traffic, sprawl, and decay. They're more than the sum of their people. How can I explain he's also fortunate to live here, to wake up every morning to a clear red sky, walking through time with every step he takes?

We round a corner along the cliff and I give a small cry.

"It's so far up," I say. "I'm glad the donkey's doing the work for me."

Rami nods. "They're more sure-footed than we are. They know exactly where to step."

"Do people ever fall?"

Rami's eyes are trained ahead, but I catch the tightness in his jawline.

"It's rare, ma'am. Don't worry."

My skin prickles. His voice carries a familiar strain, the sound of a battle between what one wants to say and what one should say. Does he know my old woman? Has he heard the story?

While I craft my next question, the donkey turns another corner and my stomach lurches. We're at the same spot where she fell. I recognize the curve of the trail, the small bush protruding into its path. I lean forward, trying to peer down the cliff.

"Can we stop for a minute?"

"Not a good place to stop, ma'am." The boy's voice is firm, tight as a knot, but I slide off the saddle and walk to the ledge.

Wind, warm under the peak sun, attacks my thinning hair. I step closer to the edge.

"Please, *sayida!*"

Switching to Arabic. I must really be stressing the boy. But I can't pull back now.

Another step, and I look down. My stomach clenches. It's there — the boulder that broke her fall. It's free of blood and gore, presumably washed clean a long time ago, but I can remember the scene as it once was, when a woman died and left her body, a witness to her own demise.

But when I lean further, my body turns rigid. I'm a rock myself, welded in place. I won't jump. I can't. I know this with a cold, brutal certainty that knocks the air from my lungs. I'm terrified of the fall. Every second feels like cool water on a parched throat. I could stand here for hours and nothing would change.

"Please." A voice cuts through the blood pounding in my ears, and I turn to meet Rami's frightened, childlike face. He offers his hand palm-up and I take it, letting myself be hoisted back onto the donkey, who chews with lazy indifference. We continue our climb as though nothing happened.

The Monastery doesn't compare to the Treasury at the base of the city, but it's impressive regardless. The surroundings more than make up for it, the horizon shimmering under the noon heat. Rami and I sit cross-legged in the shade, eating the overpriced *manaqish* I bought earlier.

"The cheese is quite good," I admit. "I don't each much these days, but I could see myself getting fat off of these."

Rami smiles. "A single family makes all of the food you can buy here. An old woman and her daughters. They sell it across the area."

I suppress commenting that the men in the family could help. I don't have the energy or the inclination —

after staring down the cliff and winning, I'm exhausted. Did I win? Had part of me hoped that I would jump as well? Now that I hadn't, I didn't know what to do next.

I say all that I can think to say. "This is a beautiful place. I don't want to be anywhere else."

Rami steals a glance at me. "There's evil here. The High Place of Sacrifice, where the Nabataeans cut animals' throats to appease their pagan gods." He gives his donkey a pat, as though reassuring it. "Battles and death. Maybe you can sense it, too. That place where you stopped? My grandmother died there."

It takes me a second to register what the young man said, the words entering my ears like thick molasses. Then my blood chills. Rami is one of her many grandchildren. It shouldn't surprise me, but this proximity to the woman's surviving kin prickles my skin, flooding my senses with shock and shame in equal measure. I terrified the boy when I leaned over the edge.

I clear my throat, gripping the sides of my dress to hide my shaking hands. "What was her name?"

He blinks, surprised. "Aisha."

A classic name. "I'm so sorry, Rami," I say. "What a terrible accident."

"She was taking a family down from the Monastery," Rami says. He doesn't correct my assumption, and I wonder if he knows what happened. "When she was younger, she hated working with the tourists. She loved to cook and preferred caring for the animals at the end of the day. But when she got older, my mother told me she loved it. She liked to learn their stories and tell her own, about her life and her family, all the things she had seen. I bet she could have written a book about all the people she met from around the world, but she never learned how to write."

I press my lips together in disbelief. A woman with a NeuroLync plugged into her temple, unable to read a book. While it could have been tradition that kept her illiterate, it was unlikely. In many ways, the Bedouin were more progressive than the urban population. Perhaps she never learned because she never needed to.

"It sounds like she had a good life," I manage.

Rami's face brightens, his dark eyes twinkling with sudden amusement. "She made everyone laugh. I read a poem once in school. It said you can't give others joy unless you carry joy in reserve, more than you need. So I know she must have been happy until the end. I believe something evil made her fall that day. It sensed that she was good. Whatever it was — a jinn, a ghost — it knew it had to defeat her."

Though exposed to modern technology and a government-run secular education, the boy had found his own mystical narrative to dampen his grief, to reason the unreasonable. *Not unlike me*, I realize. I came here in search of a secret. A special way to die, a way to secure life after death. Something unique about this place or people that would extinguish my fears. Magical thinking.

My mouth is dry. Should I tell the boy what I know from the bazaar? It would bring pain, but perhaps comfort as well. His grandmother, Aisha, died because of a strange psychological quirk, not a persuasive spirit. She was terrified but found peace in those final split seconds of the fall. She lingered somehow after meeting the ground, sinking into a warm, welcoming light. Would the boy want to know this? Would he feel betrayed by the realization that I knew about his grandmother, a stranger who had experienced her most intimate moments through a black-market bazaar?

No. Hers was not my story to tell. I'm a thief, a robber of memories, driven by my own fears. I came here for answers to a pointless question. What did it matter why she jumped? She lived well and left behind people who loved her. The people I love are far away and frantic — and yet I considered leaving them with the sight of my body splattered over rock.

As for her apparent conscious experience after death — I won't know what happened, what it meant, until it's my time. And my time isn't now, in this place. Not yet.

My face burns and I draw a shaking breath. Above me, the Monastery looms like an anchor. Through my shame, my mouth twitches in a smile. It's breathtaking. I don't regret coming here. But now, I need to go home.

"Rami, can you send a message for me with your Neuro-Lync?" I ask. My voice is hoarse but firm.

On the way back down, I close my eyes when we pass the spot on the path. I'm not afraid of jumping, but I'm afraid of the grief the jump left behind.

When we reach the base of the ruins, back at the Treasury, Rami lifts a finger to his temple.

"Your son is already in Jordan," he says. "He'll arrive here in a few hours. He says to meet him in the Mövenpick Hotel lobby."

Rami's face flushes when I kiss his forehead in gratitude, but he smiles at the generous tip I press into his hands.

I sip coffee while guests come and go through the hotel lobby. A fountain trickles a steady stream of water nearby and beautiful mosaic patterns line the walls. I'm on my third Turkish coffee when Firaz bursts through the front door.

Our eyes meet and emotions pass across his face in waves — joy, relief, fury, and exasperation. I stand up, letting him examine my face as he approaches.

"Have a seat, Firaz."

"Why are you here?" he bellows, his voice echoing across the lobby and drawing alarmed stares in our direction. Before

I can respond, he continues, "We thought you got lost and were wandering the streets," he says, back in control but still too loud for comfort. "Murdered in a ditch or dead from heatstroke. Why can't you just live, Mama? What are you trying to escape from? Were you confused? Is it the tumour?"

My poor boy, reaching for the last justification for his mad mother.

"It's not the tumour, Firaz," I say in a gentle tone. "And I wouldn't call myself confused. Lost, maybe. The tumour terrifies me, Firaz. It's not how I want to go, so I kept looking for other, better ways to make an end of everything. It was unfair to you, and I'm sorry. I really am."

Firaz groans, sinking into one of the plush seats. Massaging his temples, he closes his eyes. I give him time. It's all I can give him now. Finally, he sighs and his face softens when he faces me again. The same expression he wore when he first learned I was sick — that his mother was vulnerable in ways out of his control.

"I should have listened to you more," he says. "Asked how you were doing. Not in the superficial way — about chemo and your mood. The deeper questions. I didn't because it scares me, too. I don't want to think about you gone."

Tears prickle my eyes. "I know. I don't want to leave you, either. For a while, I thought dying would be doing you a favour. But nothing is more important to me than you, Firaz. That won't change, even if this tumour starts frying every part of my brain. I'll love you until my last breath. I want to spend my last months with you and Reema, if you'll have me."

Silence follows. We sit together for an hour, letting the world hum around us, before Firaz finally stands up.

"How did you know to fly to Jordan, before my guide contacted you?"

I ask when we reach the Wadi Musa train station. We board the day's last train together.

Firaz's mouth forms a grim, triumphant line. "Reema did some digging around at the Underground Bazaar. Grilled all the staff there about what you watched, and questions you asked. She pieced together that you probably ran off to Petra."

"She's resourceful," I say with a grin. "You were smart to marry her.

After I go — "

"Mom!"

"After I go," I continue, "I want you both to live the lives you desire. Move for that perfect job. Travel. Eat that sugary dessert on the menu. Find little moments of joy. I mean it, Firaz. Don't be afraid. If I've learned one thing from all of this, it's that sometimes you need to leap. Whatever awaits us at the end, it seems to be somewhere warm and safe. Even if it's followed by nothing, we have nothing to fear from death."

Anguish tightens Firaz's face, but after a moment, something inside of him appears to release and his eyes shine with understanding. He helps me into a seat at the back of the train carriage.

"Let's go home."

I catch a final glimpse of Wadi Musa's white buildings, uneven like jagged teeth, as the train pulls away. Past the town, Petra's hills run together, freckled by dark dwellings. It's bleak but beautiful, and I close my eyes to burn the scene into my memory. I want to remember everything.

A DAY IN THE LIFE OF ANMAR 20X1

by Abdulla Moaswes

Abdulla is a Palestinian writer, educator, researcher, and translator. He was once named the world's foremost scholar of chai karak by a prestigious research centre's Twitter account, and he maintains a keen interest in modern Arabic and Urdu poetry. For a decade during his childhood, he went to school next door to the famous Sharjah Cricket Stadium and he remains—among a small group of people who do not know one another—deeply committed to the revival of Palestinian cricket. You can find him on Twitter as @KarakMufti.

It was 10 a.m., and Anmar clapped his hands to silence the screeching wake-up alarm he had set for himself. He didn't actually *need* the alarm, since he had already been awake for twelve minutes before it went off, but Anmar enjoyed using technology whenever he could, even if he didn't need it (his staff would say *especially* when he didn't need it). In fact, he prided himself on how technology had made his oh-so-important job oh-so-much-easier and efficient.

Anmar could have woken up earlier. He could have woken up later. He had developed a habit of waking up during the mid-to-late morning during his days as a technology entrepreneur. It accustomed him to a most irregular schedule, in which he did most of his work during the night or whenever he felt like it, really. Of course, he did not extend this luxury to his diligent employees. Anmar, of course, had unique gifts from the higher powers that meant that he could *only* operate efficiently in this way and—therefore—that only *he* could operate in this way.

These days, Anmar proudly serves his country as the President of the Palestinian Authority. He was (s)elected to lead the Authority when he was quite young (for a world leader), and he is currently serving the 11th year of his constitutionally defined four-year term, as has become tradition among the esteemed Presidents of the Palestinian Authority. Under his leadership, the primary objective of his administration has been to safeguard the territorial integrity of the State of Palestine. So far, Anmar has been quite satisfied with the progress his administration has achieved in this regard, if he may say so himself! (And one can believe that he frequently does say it—himself.)

After silencing the screeching alarm that he programmed to ring throughout the house, Anmar disembarked from his thermo-modulated bed and went into his en suite restroom to release his bowels into the complex network of subterranean pipes and wires that kept his Estate running with relative self-sufficiency. Anmar cared deeply for matters of sustainability and environmental protection. Of course, it was necessary for him to care since it did, after all, help him gain the approval of the powers that granted him his job.

Many individuals of considerable importance considered it a priority that the next President of the Palestinian Authority represent a departure from the crusty, old-world-minded bureaucrats and reformed revolutionaries of old. Anmar, in both his professional background and political worldview, represented both change and realism, and he bore a pragmatic optimism rooted in his knowledge of the wonders of science—an unorthodox but potent concoction when it came to crafting the sort of persona that the (s)electorate believed should lead the Palestinian Authority into the uncertain future. It also helped that Anmar's ripening within the technology industry meant that his personal networks were strong in both Washington, DC and Beijing.

Following his timely release, Anmar casually strolled into his kitchen, where Radi, his personal chef, awaited him. Radi was a state-of-the-art piece of culinary hardware and intelligence—Anmar's favourite, in fact, because it reminded him that, although he could not assemble an intelligent meal himself, he could assemble the necessary intelligence required to assemble one on his behalf!

With a sprawling smile invading his face, Anmar put a polite demand to his chef: "Radi, prepare breakfast! And kindly be sure to use the Italian olive oil and Turkish labneh, please. I am in a great mood this morning!"

Anmar had printed a quote from a former senior Palestinian negotiator onto the wide windows of his kitchen, where he enjoyed having meals when eating in private: "Negotiating in pain and frustration for five years is cheaper than exchanging bullets for five minutes."

His staff were unsure whether the quote was meant to be an optimistic reminder of Anmar's commitment to peace or a macabre dismissal of the collective pain that continued to befall Palestinians in the decades that were allowed to take place between the present day and the Oslo Accords. Although the spirit and rationale of the quote remained clear to Anmar, his staff were less confident about its value after the tens of years of negotiations as opposed to the aforementioned five.

Anmar's house was situated in the centre of what many would consider a vast estate, though it was a bit of a downgrade from Anmar's previous residence in Silicon Valley. Nevertheless, as the proud President of the Palestinian Authority, Anmar was prepared to make sacrifices for the cause—especially since many areas within the West Bank kept getting cordoned off as special security zones. In fact, the Presidential Estate where he lived and rarely ever left— with its high-tech central housing unit, adjoining service wing, and gloriously sprawling grounds (within Palestinian limits)—accounted for a large part of what was currently the sovereign territory of the State of Palestine and was serviced by an inordinately large number of "essential staffers," as Anmar referred to them. It was the largest contiguous part of the territory and Anmar resolved to ensure that no encroachments could be made upon it—as a service to his people, of course!

Anmar had insisted that the house be surrounded by large windows that looked outward upon the Estate's grounds. From where he sat, enjoying every bite of his breakfast before his kitchen's big windows, all one could see were rolling green hills and picturesque plains, perhaps a village or two in the far distance. In the nearer distance, there may have been a couple of houses resembling the President's own.

Anmar revelled in the beauty, for it was one of his proudest creations. It was a brilliant canvas of greens and natural colours that defined what made the Palestinian landscapes so brilliant and desirable and what had inspired such serenity in the hearts of generation upon generation of farmers of this land—all put together by a complex system of mirrors and large screens lining the inside of the physical walls that encircled the Estate. Anmar called the technology PaleStimulate, and in his view, it was the most outstanding expression of his excellence as an innovator.

Naturally, as someone who made his start as an important entrepreneur, Anmar was not one to spend any time wasting time. Anmar practiced what he programmed, and one of the most fundamental functions he programmed into his devices was the ability to multitask. As he savoured his breakfast, he received important updates from many of the staff members who lived on his Estate.

"Good morning, Asad!" Anmar exclaimed as his most trusted Chief of Estate Staff entered the kitchen. "What good news do you have for me today?"

"Well, as you know, as of the start of February we find ourselves in the middle of the uncomfortably warm season," replied Asad, using "uncomfortably warm" as a euphemism for "scorching hot to the point of provoking the prolific use of profanity."

"Therefore, the grounds staff thank you for the kind generosity you have extended toward them by obliging them to live within the boundaries of the Estate, away from their loved ones in less commodious locales," he continued, careful to not use the term *walls*.

Anmar had built PaleStimulate to ensure that no unsightly walls were visible from inside the property. He absolutely detested walls; in fact, there was nothing he hated more. The sight of them triggered a kind of sickness in the pit of his belly that more often than not transformed into a debilitating rage.

"You are a good man and a blessing, Asad!" Anmar responded. "Thank you for delivering this fine news. This is why you are my most loyal and dedicated employee!"

Asad was half a generation older than the President and possessed a clear memory of the days before his rule. He remembered when it was possible for the man holding the office of President to leave his palace and work from a government building somewhere in Ramallah. In fact, he rather longed for those days since, although they were not significantly more dignified than the present, at least then he did not have to layer his disdain for the current order with facetiousness during every one of the President's waking hours.

Asad regarded his new sardonic tone and latent impudence as a form of everyday resistance. It was his take on the Palestinian tradition of sumud, informed by a close reading of Machiavelli's *The Prince*.

No sooner had Asad concluded his report than the Estate's Central Operating System began broadcasting nationalistic but affectively sterile Palestinian music which only the peace-loving Palestinian Authority could have commissioned for production in recent years.

"We have such a rich tradition of resistance music, Mr. President. Why do you insist on having these awful tracks play when receiving holocalls from our *friends*?" asked Asad, placing emphasis on the final word to indicate disapproval.

"Well, my dear Asad, most of the popular songs may come across as antagonistic, and that is not the mindset I want to use when speaking to our negotiating partners, of course!" Anmar replied. "Besides, I like listening to songs that celebrate the achievement of our State. It's good for morale!"

Anmar, forgetting (or ignoring the fact) that he was still in his pyjamas, picked up the call by banging his fist on the table where he ate his breakfast, summoning a hologram of Eitay, a senior member of the Israeli negotiating team. Eitay was a grizzled veteran negotiator, and his demeanour demanded complete respect from those he spoke to, despite his overly broad smile.

"Eitay! I see you are as well-dressed as usual, despite it just being the start of the day," exclaimed Anmar, with a matching smile. "To what do I owe the pleasure of your company this morning?"

"Mister Anmar, firstly, it is almost noon," Eitay began. "And secondly, I am calling you today to discuss important business. We have recently received reports from our Defence Forces about incidents of Palestinian citizens living illegally within our security enclaves and enclosures. While we do not accuse you of anything ill-intentioned, we seek to remind you of your responsibilities under the Security Coordination Accords of 20X0, which stipulate that the transfer of all citizens of the Palestinian Authority to areas marked and zoned for their legal dwelling is the responsibility of the entity that you are currently the President of."

"I see—" started Anmar, with all the coolness that one would expect from a man in his esteemed position. His memory had almost touched the Accords the negotiator mentioned, signed some years ago in one of the Gulf capitals Anmar visited on his frequent tours of the region, before Eitay continued his statement uninterrupted.

"Of course, as an initial measure of compensation, we are withholding some of the tax revenue collected from your citizens. In addition, we will require financial reparations, amounting to a significant amount of the aid monies that your Authority continues to receive from the international community. We have had to increase surveillance within those enclosures and enclaves due to the presence of the citizens illegally present there."

"Will that be all you demand?" asked Anmar, pondering how Palestinian citizens were able to infiltrate said security enclaves and enclosures. As far as Anmar knew, they were impenetrable, and the only way for Palestinians to exist within them is for them to have already been there when they were cordoned off!

"For now? Yes. But we should warn you that if you do not hand over the funds and commit to a timely transfer of your citizens, we will be forced to annex more of the land claimed by your Authority," Eitay replied. "I make this demand somewhat reluctantly, in my personal capacity. However, in my capacity as a negotiator I must reiterate that we must ensure the primacy of our own state's security, and if you cannot be trusted to make this assurance, then we must do it ourselves. We expect your response within the afternoon."

And before Anmar was able to ask any further questions, Eitay's likeness faded into nothingness, leaving behind only a sharp air of tension.

"Surely you cannot capitulate to these demands, Sir!" shouted Asad in an uncharacteristic break from his usual stoic calm. Anmar, though surprised by the outburst, smiled softly.

"My dear Asad, as a people we are quite wealthy, and surely I can raise the necessary funds through my flagship Citizen's Solidarity Fund to protect the territorial integrity of our state," explained the President, referencing his pseudomicrotaxation programme which exacted what he saw as small amounts from the electronic financial transactions of low-earning Palestinians. "Now that we have finally developed a workaround to collect some of our own tax income, which our friends have yet to protest, our advisors stationed in several friendly states have suggested we find ways to benefit from the disproportionately large low-earner demographic among our citizenry. Surely, we designed it for instances such as this, when our state's sovereignty is threatened!"

"If I may humbly make a suggestion—" Asad began, falling back into a more reserved and euphemistic way of speaking. "Would you not stand to benefit by speaking directly to the poor families who live on the land in question that Eitay spoke of? Perhaps they might be able to offer some insight? Or at least offer a potential way out of this political quandary?"

"Don't be ridiculous!" retorted the President. "Such an approach could endanger our position vis-à-vis Eitay and his team! We pay our advisors a lion's share of our national budget to offer us solutions to exactly such problems, and we trust the firms they represent to ensure we only work with the very best minds when it comes to conflict resolution. Speaking to those who caused this crisis is a reckless approach to safeguarding our national interests, and we can't be seen buckling to populist overtures that may put those interests at risk—like the Boycott campaign, to name one example, or your proposal, to name another! We will follow the agreed-upon accords and protocols, pay what we owe, and request that the relevant authorities manage the situation on the ground."

With that, Asad took leave of his employer and resigned himself to his dimly lit office in the service wing of the Estate, rolling his eyes perilously as he turned his back to leave Anmar's kitchen.

It did not really matter that he did it outside of Anmar's sight since the President was too preoccupied to notice anyway. He was busy dictating an order of coffee using an overly complex preparation method to Chef Radi, as he enjoyed sipping on gourmet synthetic coffees while making deals with Eitay.

Mimicking the face-to-face coffee meetings of old, during the times before the coffee bean was wiped out by the Great Rubiaceous Plague, gave him a most empowered feeling of sophistication and confidence. He felt that this feeling was a necessary part of a successful negotiation from the perspective of the Palestinian Authority.

President Anmar then called Eitay, whose likeness again occupied the vacant space designated for holocalls, to deliver his highly deliberated-upon decision and, in his view, save the State of Palestine in the process.

"We are grateful for your cooperation and respect for our agreements. Therefore, we will accept the monetary compensation owed, and I will implore my team to allow the authorities to manage the situation on the ground. Thank you, President Anmar, for indeed, you are a credit to your people."

Not much else of note happened that day. Aside from averting a politically problematic position while safeguarding the interests of his Authority, Anmar did command his staff to repair a faulty PaleStimulate screen.

While on a run by the outer perimeter of the Presidential Estate, Anmar was saddened to discover a dull grey piece of wall before him. The panel meant to hide it did not appear to be damaged, so Anmar, with his technological genius, determined that the issue was most likely in its power supply. The sadness triggered by this glimpse of the wall ripped through his soul like a bullet through cotton and linen fibre paper.

"MAINTENANCE!" yelled Anmar, whose voice carried through the sonic nervous system he had installed within the Estate to ensure that his orders were heard by staff members at all times. "I see a wall before me on the outer perimeter!"

Of course, Anmar did not need to mention his exact location, for as he had expected, the portion of PaleStimulate suffering a power failure was clear to see in the master control room, and a team of technicians was dispatched at once to diagnose the problem.

"Mr. President, it seems to us that the underground wires powering this panel have been damaged by an overgrowth of a cactus root," the lead technician stated. "The actual cactus stands a few feet outside the boundary."

"Well then, uproot the damn cactus and restore power to the panel!" the President demanded. His eyes were irrationally bloodshot and his face red with rage.

"Sir, we are unable to uproot the cactus," started the technician, "for it falls outside of the boundary, and we are not allowed to set foot there."

While the words of the technician were technically true, modern agricultural technology had devised systems that allowed for the remote uprooting of cacti. It might have even been developed in joint collaboration between Anmar's firm and an Israeli one, in a move that might have been presented to the world as a step towards peace; however, the President, in his furious and frenzied state, was in no position to recall this.

The lead technician did not remind him of this technology that would allow them to uproot their beloved stolen homeland's cacti, despite the words of protocols, accords, and unpopular agreements.

"I did not hire you to tell me about what you cannot do!" Anmar snapped back. "Find a way to restore power and hide this painful eyesore no matter the cost!"

Ultimately, a temporary solution was found to restore the serene visual the President had become so accustomed to laying his eyes upon during the arduous hours of his most important work. It is necessary that he be able to think with a clear head when running the Authority that was fighting for a legitimate Palestinian state.

The technicians discovered a way to re-wire the panels to reconstruct the normal order, but they warned him the continued and unrestrained growth of roots would one day attack the system in far more substantial ways.

"When may this occur?" Anmar asked meekly, his soul comforted by the return of beautiful scenery and the disappearance of the gruesome grey that ruined his evening.

"We forecast its occurrence in the distant future, but one can never predict such things with certainty. Just as we were unable to foresee this incident despite all the expertise and technology available to us, as well as your visionary involvement."

Anmar, pleased with the results of his technicians' labour and comforted by the projection that more substantial failures would occur when he likely no longer occupied the Presidential Estate, was glad to wave away the warnings and continue with his evening routine.

Late into the night, as he lay his head upon his pillow, Anmar cycled through the events of the day that had just passed. It was an unremarkable day, with nothing but a routine set of problems for a man in his esteemed position to solve. All things considered, both his negotiation with Eitay and his leadership in fixing the PaleStimulate system were great victories, and Anmar liked victories. In one day, he had both maintained the territorial integrity of the Palestinian State and the dependability of his otherworldly technological innovations!

Upon arriving at the end of those reflections, Anmar congratulated himself on yet another successful day as the President of the Palestinian Authority. He then fought the insomniac excitement brought about by the opportunity to confront bigger and more credible challenges in the coming days, weeks, months, and years, closed his eyes, and went to sleep.

Cinnamon Flavour Gum

by Maria Dadouch

Translation by Simone Noto

Maria Dadouch is a Syrian author, born in Damascus, in 1970. She received a degree in Creative Writing in 2015 from the University of California at Los Angeles (ULSC). She helped found the magazine "Fulla" in 2005, on which she wrote many articles and stories until 2012. She also worked as a screenwriter for the famous TV comedy series Maraya. *When the war broke out in Syria, Maria Dadouch moved to the United States. She has published 4 novels and many children's books, some of which have been translated into English, including* Omar and Oliver. *In 2018, her novel* The Planet of Uncertainties *won the Katara Prize. In 2019, she won the Shoman Prize for the science fiction novel* I Want Golden Eyes. *In 2020 she won the Arab Publishers Forum Prize for the book* Him and I.

As I sit in the waiting room, I am surrounded by elderly people on all sides. We sit in rows of and a heavy cloud of waiting hovers over us. At any moment, the virtual secretary will appear and call one of our numbers to take that person through the metal door on the other side of the room. The secretary's legs are too long and thin and she also has the same provocative white teeth as Nadia, the secretary of the gym club that I go to. Yesterday, Nadia suggested that I run on the top of the Icelandic mountains or walk on the shores of Lake Logan, but I ended up running towards the Dubai desert, angry about her bright teeth. After the secretary reappears and calls number 111, we all heave a sigh of relief, except for number 111, of course. Although he pretends to be brave he is betrayed by his clumsy steps and curved shoulders. My number is 144, so they're going to call 33 more wretches before my time comes. There is a gap of three or four minutes between the exit of one unhappy person and the next, meaning I have roughly a hundred minutes ahead of me... a hundred minutes before a virtual secretary calls me, a hundred minutes before my life ends.

Of course, I didn't tell Anissa, my wife, that I was coming here today, here to the "Official Center for the Blessing of Human Organs". On the day I signed the contract to end my life, earlier this year, Anissa pleaded with me not to tell her beforehand of the day I decided to end my life because she would not be able to say goodbye.

"I can't live without you", she said. She always says that, and many other kind words and then she forces me, for instance, to eat a buffalo cheese sandwich without heating it, as she fears the cheese will melt on the metal plate and she will have to clean it. She says I am the most important thing in her life, but then she forgets my favourite white robe in a UV sterilizer. High-absorption boron nitrite nanosheets were provided as a gift with the last camera I bought. Two hours after going into the sterilizer, both came out toasted and dark. Anissa said something like that to me this morning. She said – "I do not want to wake up in the morning and find you are not in bed with me" – then, she scolded me for always wetting the toilet seat when I flushed after urinating. She says that she would have wet her clothes if she hadn't taken ten seconds to dry the toilet seat (my fault) before using it. She claims that her bladder got weaker with each of the three pregnancies she went through to give me our children. However, aside from her bladder, my wife's vital organs are not in good health. Here at the "Official Center for the Blessing of Human Organs", children are given two doses of anti-virus vaccine for every six perfectly functioning organs donated. Our children are lucky, I am able to donate excellent organs and this will this ensure they will receive the necessary vaccine doses. A virtual secretary who looks like a muscled man appears a few rows back and whispers to a woman with exceptionally wide hips: "Number 119? Come with me". The lady responds and heads towards the metal door with her companion. Her hijab is elegantly decorated with light purple roses. I didn't dress well today, I was smart and wore old clothes. I put on some old clothes because they will wrap me in white Egyptian cotton, and I am sure they will throw away my clothes as soon as they take them off. I was lucky because this month they added a new free service called "Ghusl Kafan".[2] I am Muslim, and this is clearly the reason why; whereas Christians are given a free coffin made of hardened and waterproof polyamide wood. Not every-one has this advantage, but they have been generous with me because most of my organs, such as the spleen, pancreas, prostate, eyes, and thyroid are exceptional. My ears can hear all the waves at 10 decibels. What else? Kidneys ... yeah, even those. My urine is as pure as gold, and in exchange for those organs, I easily obtained a legal contract guaranteeing me two sealed boxes containing enough vaccine doses for my twin daughters, with an expiration date ending in 2076. But for the brother of the twins... it was much more difficult to get his doses. The Center of Human Organs representative I signed the contract with was an expert, like all the other

---

2 Ghusl, also known as "sacred washing", is an Arabic term used to describe the process Muslims have to go through in order to restore purity before Allah. Kafan, instead, is a term used to describe the shroud that wraps a Muslim's body after purification, directing him to the mosque and the sacred city of Mecca.

representatives, and obviously he tried to avoid giving me vaccines for my son too. The BlindVid-55 vaccine is very expensive, according to pharmaceutical companies.

I said to him, "Would you be willing to accept that the BlindVid-55 virus infected my son and caused him to lose his sight, while his two sisters were still able to enjoy their sight until the last day of their lives? Put yourself in my shoes, would you?"

He said that it was my fault and yelled, "You have three kids when there are only two of you? Don't you know that today's birth rate is three fetuses per every four and a half people? Four, not two.

A second virtual secretary interrupted my thoughts, and I didn't know if it was a man or a woman, who jumped up and grabbed a big man who occupied the last two seats in my row. Did he say number 128? Is it possible for all these people have gone so quickly? When the "Blessing of Human Organs" representative reminded me about the current reproductive rate I didn't have an answer. What could I say? Should I tell him that my government's signing of the international fuel rationing agreement has caused me to have so many children? Since the sale of heating devices that utilize renewable energy has been monopolized by large technology companies and sold at exorbitant prices there has been no other way to stay warm except to embrace under the quilt? Thereafter, with a slip of the tongue, the representative found out that my children had come naturally out of my wife's womb, and he almost passed out. Licking his lips and rubbing his palms, he said: "I will give you doses of your child's vaccine and doses for another person to sell on your behalf, if you persuade your wife to end her life with you".

Of course, I declined, but he began to beg and plead with me. He said uteri that have not undergone a C-section are rare, and their sale is guaranteed. Male cooks are the most common surrogacy clients because it makes motherhood easier. Chefs cook their dishes live on Calaxi-Net, and the presence of pregnant chefs suggests motherhood to their followers, so their tendency is to convince themselves that their dishes are delicious, which results in an increase in their net rating. A chef who is highly regarded can easily a good job in one of the houses or restaurants of the Techno-Emperors Island. I obviously didn't accept because I didn't want Anissa to sign an end-of-life contract. She won't need it if I can only guarantee vaccine doses for our children. I kept going and negotiated with him over my liver and heart. I told him: "I do not smoke, I do not drink alcohol or take drugs, my heart and liver are like they just left the factory". But he started to bring to my attention the worn-out joints in my knees and hips, the enlarged prostate, and the laziness of my... my... important organ... he was humming and humming, but I was not going to give up, not when Anissa's life was at stake. I threw the documentation of my spine and neck that I had kept until the end in front of him, and only then did the evil person submit to me. There was not a single kink in the vertebrae of my neck and back, obviously because of my being a photographer. This is almost the only advantage of the photographer's profession. Due to the emergence of the "hyena neck", the erect neck is rare in this period, which is caused by leaning on their own holobionts. His jaw dropped and he was open mouthed in disbelief when I showed him the model of my spine that I had had printed that morning with a high-precision 3D printer. As soon as he saw it, he immediately added my son's vaccine to the contract. Resignedly, he pointed the iris scanner at me and said: "You beat me. You have just won the lifetime contract that everyone dreams of. Oh Allah, he fell into the apple of your eye, you are lucky with the blessing of Allah".

And I gave in.

Yeah, I signed it.

They call number 133, the man with that number goes with the secretary and disappears behind the metal door.

What choice did I have but to sign? I am not very excited about ending my life, there are many things I long for God to extend my life for. I left behind television bubble where the heroes of the latest episode of the series "Horror on Mars" are hiding. I paused the series while they were about to depart the reserve, unaware of the guards. I intentionally didn't watch the last episode as it was likely that the guards would target them and their blood would spill on the tiles of the television screen, and my heart couldn't handle the sadness any more. Photographing the northern lights before I die is something I've wanted to do since I was a child. Upon becoming a professional photographer, I carefully planned the photo: My dream was to work for no pay as a photographer on the "ice submarine of my dreams" that would take me to the South Pole. I planned my dream step by step: going to the platform before sunset bringing with me a large camera memory and spare batteries, all charged, ready to observe the northern lights. I focus the camera on the tripod, utilize a wide-angle lens, and adjust it for high and low lighting to gather the greatest possible amount of light. I choose a bright star and use it to focus. Next, I wait for the northern lights to appear and determine their speed. Finally, adjusting the shutter speed accordingly, I let the camera do its amazing job, and I enjoy it, watching this extraordinary cosmic phenomenon.

I am about to leave the world without accomplishing this dream. All right, I haven't been worried about my dreams much lately, but Anissa... I wish, by God, I could buy Anissa the platinum bracelet from the three-dimensional image on my phone on the eve of every wedding anniversary. Anissa believes that I think this advertisement pops up at random and was brought to my attention by pure coincidence with the ads of that day, but I know very well that she sent it from her ball to mine through a special application that allows her to do so. Anissa didn't ask for anything every year because she always asked for that bracelet. I swear I wish I had bought it for her, but the eye sees further than where Bitcoins can reach.[3] The important thing is ... I wish I didn't have to sign that contract. Since the predatory virus appeared 20 years ago, a poor man like me, if he loves his children, can't *not* sign any more. The virus can make you blind within a few hours. You have healthy eyes and use your cell phone's alarm clock to wake you up at dawn and call you to prayer. After that, you become aware that this alarm is the last image your eyes will ever see. The problem isn't just about the loss of vision, but also about the distance between you and everyone else. You are ostracized by them due to your contagiousness. My mother always said, "You are more precious than my eyes"; but it turns out that this is not true, because nothing is more precious than your eyes. The proof is that your family members are the first to let you down. Who can blame your wife and kids? They will notify the security personnel right away to arrest you; you'll be snatched by nylon pliers and thrown into the asylum, which is actually a human landfill: no one visits patients, and no one comes in to provide for their needs except for a few employees. How miserable is that employee who agrees to do this dangerous job; a job in an asylum for patients suffering from the BlindVid-55. The staff give

---

3 The reference is to the Arabic proverb "العين ترى أبعد من اليد" (the eye sees farther than the hand).

the patients packaged food in one hand and a lot of anger and frustration in the other. They only work for two hours, then abandon the rest of their shift to reduce their exposure time to the virus. They run to the sterilizer then quickly leave that bleak building. The asylum building has mould covering it and lacks any sanitary facilities, there are only communal dormitories, and dirt. Videos of the asylum are leaking into our wandering balls daily. While watching a video about the bathrooms there, I once imagined my twin daughters blind and growing up in that place. So, at once I threw myself without hesitation in the arms of the representative of the "Center of Human Organs" asking him to sign a closer document – a life contract with me so I can get vaccines for my children. I watched a video this morning that showed a group of patients trying to escape: but how can you escape from all those high electrified fences and sirens? What if you are ill or weak? Or blind?

I hear the number 142 echoing behind me as my turn is approaching. I won't be upset; I made the right decision, and my children will be able to enjoy their sight for the rest of their lives. My hope is that they will be grateful, but unfortunately, this wish won't come true because they won't remember me. I have worked tirelessly to pay for their expenses, and they haven't expressed their gratitude during my life, so why should they be grateful to me after death?

Throughout my work days, I spend my time in the arms of the bridge between the Emperor's Island of Technology and the Island of Compassionate Medicine, wandering from one resort to another, begging luxury guests to let me take their picture. I tempt them by saying that the traditional camera hanging from my neck produces images that are unique and unlike modern ones. Sometimes they accept, and other times, when the end of the day is approaching and I am not going to be able to buy any food, I hide in a sheltered area and watch the people around, me waiting for the right moment to take what I call the "opportunistic photo". A secretary with her manager, for instance, with her hand resting in a place where it is not allowed, or two fancy girls exchanging obscene words that we only hear in suspended subway stations. The owners of these snapshots generously pay me to delete them so that they do not find their way to Galaxy-Net. It is clear to me that taking these opportunistic photos is not a good way to behave, sometimes I received a generous amount of money to delete them and left with a bloated Bitcoin card, able to pay my bills until the end of the week. I can't deny it has not always been smooth sailing, and the owners of those photos sometimes called security men to throw me out of the resort. On those days I came home with wounds and bruises. Did my children worry about my miserable condition at that moment? No, they never did.

I would enter the house, and nobody would say hello. Anissa is usually at work when I get back. I can't even talk to her about my concerns. Her task is to find with precision an opening in the clouds so that the new green taxi-copter the Nahla-Bot Company gave her can be launched and landed, any distraction could lead to an unfortunate accident, so what should I do? I jump on the couch, put on the VR helmet, start a beginner-level boxing game, hitting my opponent with my fists. This is what I do. During the break between games, they used to wipe my sweat with a handkerchief, give me water, and hold my shoulders. I wish I had never taken off my helmet. *How do you feel when someone touches your tired muscles?* Anyway, what matters is that upon finishing playing and taking off my helmet, I see my two daughters struggling with the small creature they were given prolactin for, and they nursed him to make him their pet. By breastfeeding, they feel maternal towards their adopted child. They chose the colour and shape of his eyes from the infant Orphan Hospital catalogue and adopted him. They told me and their mother they don't have to get married any more because they have a child already.

Their generation boasts about the intelligent solutions they have created for common problems, and they say marriage always ends in divorce. May God forgive them for adding a new mouth I had to feed, as if I need another.

Even their brother is not better than them. He spent four months working on Amazon balloons where he was in charge of sending remote-controlled planes to delivery addresses. What did he do with his salary? He bought his TV bubble (which became his room): he covered the windows and didn't open the door (except for the bathroom), not even to get his mother's food tray. Parents are like that; they always make sacrifices, and their children are reckless. My father also signed an end-of-life contract 20 years ago, so I am lucky enough to still be able to see. On the day of his death, he felt nostalgia for the days of the Covid-19 virus which he had experienced in his youth and only caused severe flu. My father sacrificed himself for me, and I will do the same, and that's the rule of life. On the day I buried my father, I had to go to the labour market, but is that what my children will do tomorrow, after they receive my corpse, frowning like Frankenstein's monster, and bury me? I am not sure. I'll stop worrying about them.

Everyone reaps what they sow. My current worry is whether Allah will forgive me for signing my end-of-life contract. All divine religions forbid suicide, and I am seriously afraid that the contract to end one's life is considered suicide in the eyes of Allah. Some Sheiks give sermons on Fridays and say that this is permissible, but those who do not receive their salary from the government say the opposite, and today I really hope they are wrong. A female voice next to me is saying "Number 144".

I open my eyes and see the virtual secretary standing next to me, I notice the metal door is open behind her.

The secretary says, "Mr. 144, your bed is ready. On the small tray attached to it, you will find the chewing gum to end your life with, there are different flavours. They just added cinnamon flavour gum, aren't you lucky? Do you like cinnamon?"

To New Jerusalem

By Farah Kader

Farah Kader is Palestinian American. She has a BA in Public Health from the University of California Berkeley and an MPH from the University of Michigan. Farah was a recipient of the 2017 Palestinian Youth Movement's Ghassan Kanafani Writing Prize and a 2019 Hopwood Graduate Award for poetry. Her work has been published in Mizna, Orion Magazine, Electric Literature, and Narrative Magazine. Farah currently works in New York as a public health analyst.

The backseat passenger sits up straight on the side opposite the driver with her hands folded in her lap. Her eyes are hard with disquiet as they stare through the side window to the infinite smudge that a passing cityscape becomes. The driver maintains a steady speed, accelerating only to give his battered taxi enough momentum to skid over any holes in the pavement. There is no parallel traffic, radio static, or sounds of breathing to puncture the stillness inside this capsule, just the staccato rumblings of a waning engine.

She feels comfortable enough to rest against the seat back now. The passenger presses her shoulder blades into the cushion, which is softer than she anticipates as it absorbs all of her weight. This glimpse of calm is cut by the sudden awareness of cigarette residue clinging to the air around her. She has been tasting it since she first opened the taxi door several minutes ago, but now she processes all her senses. The miasma elicits girlhood, when visits to the Submerged were as common as shop tobacco.

It occurs to the passenger that this vehicle is another relic of the Submerged and must have held thousands of satisfied exhales, the upholstery absorbing thousands of puffs of smoke in its history. The driver, still silent, may have once or twice sat alone in his taxi for hours, watching the tides come in and out, waiting for a passenger for days, weeks, immersed in his own exhaust. She envisions all that fabric plumped by a decades-long stream of thick, ashy vapor. This was the vice for those who knew the future and did not care to stay long for it.

The passenger is anxious again, holding her breath tightly. It is ingrained in all residents of the Sanctuary Cities that items such as cigarettes and personal vehicles will one day bring the same fate to the Cities as they did the Submerged. The passenger imagines that if she peeks down at the floor mats, she will find her soles resting atop a mound of cigarette buds and looks upward to avoid such a fate.

The driver lifts his head to see a tightly cropped image of her face in the rear-view mirror. There are flecks of mascara pressed along her orbital bone. Sleeplessness makes her blinking slow. The passenger shifts her attention from the window to the rear-view mirror, seeing the driver's eyes and forehead, wrinkled with leather-like skinfolds stacked beneath a low, bristly hairline.

"You shouldn't be here by yourself," he says. "It's dangerous for people who don't know where they're going."

His lips barely touch as he speaks. The sounds between vowels emerge muffled, thrust from the back of the throat rather than the tongue. There is something in this voice that ignites nostalgia in her, but she brushes that aside, feeling her face fill with tension. Glaring into the rear-view mirror, she responds, "I'm actually very familiar with the area, but thanks for your concern."

The driver shrugs and continues to look straight ahead. She knows her response is too formal, even uppity. He is older than her, but not by much. She considers explaining herself, that she is not just another tourist, one of those adventurers who view the Submerged as one does a fossil. Those who never had to bear witness to the destruction of something so vast, something they loved.

The States Parties to this Convention,

Recognizing the considerable pace at which sea levels rise, coastal zones sink, water reduces in availability, desertification spreads, and hydro-meteorological disasters reoccur at present,

Acknowledging that the stresses of global climate change are compounded by human overpopulation and over consumption of natural resources,

Considering there are great risks stemming from population pressure and mass displacement by natural and manmade forces, particularly on those facing social and environmental vulnerability,

Having in mind that, in accordance with existing human rights law, all human beings have the right to a national home and a standard of living adequate for health and well-being,

Believing that preservation of cultural heritage and wildlife conservation must also be priorities,

Noting that States are responsible for the safety, well-being, and protection of internally displaced citizens,

Emphasizing that those who are currently stateless or unable to remain in their home countries due to crowding, warfare, persecution, and other crises exacerbated by the global climate,

Have agreed as follows:

More things that the passenger remembers: brownstones, scaffolding, Art Deco, other taxis. Maybe the endurance of cigarette stench brought on these recollections. In the last taxi, she was eight, squished between her father and two strangers in the back seat, her pregnant mother in the front, directing the driver in garbled Arabic to go, go quickly, now.

"There aren't many left," her uncle had told her, back when she revealed she would make the trip back, "but they will be your only option if you want to reach New Jerusalem."

Although many memories come to her now, in her restless state, the passenger has forgotten how the taxi arrived or how she got in.

Her phone is unusable here, otherwise she would have seen the driver's name and photo flash across her screen with a countdown to his arrival time. She would have paused at the wide eyes and bumpy nose and dense brows. He would have confirmed her identity when he pulled onto the curb, and perhaps the exchange of names would have answered some of their unspoken questions, the possible chain links that connected them to this part of the Submerged. But she did not know his name, and he did not know hers.

There are still at least 45 minutes left of the hour-long drive, she surmises. The fractured road keeps their bodies bouncing in unison. She and the driver both direct their attention to the monochromatic landscape that stretches endlessly forward. A wide, white crevice of sky pushes apart brick and slate on either side of the street, then tapers to a narrow sliver at the horizon line. The passenger reaches into the pocket of her jacket and endeavours to unfold her map without sound. The crinkling paper betrays her.

"What is your name?" the driver asks.

She can tell from the way he poses the question that it is one of many questions he keeps stored at the ready, one of those calibrating questions that gets closer to the real question. Depending on who does the asking, it can be *are you one of us?* or, more often, *are you one of them?*

His inkling may be based on her appearance, some of the features that keep her tied to all the Submerged her ancestors saw drown before this one. He has them too. Of course, she knows from all her time in the Sanctuary Cities that phenotypes are misleading. They are false ties to lands lost, stereotypes of old that humans carry in bundles to the outermost bounds of their ignorance. But his accent, like cigarettes, are remnants of the past.

The passenger gives the driver her name. Like confronted with an epiphany, he exclaims, "Ah-ha! I married a lady with this name!"

He lifts his hand and smacks the steering wheel. The passenger waits to hear more about the lady, but it seems this revelation has satisfied his curiosity.

"Does she ever come here with you?" she asks.

"No, we came here together. Long time ago. But she went back." He waves his hand as if to indicate the general direction in which she went.

"To the Sanctuaries?"

"No, to Jaffa."

"Jaffa is Submerged now. How could she go back?"

"She went back before it went under. She thought maybe there would still be a place for her, but of course they sent her to the camps."

"And then what?"

"She was in Yarmouk, and then we lost touch. I know her family was there. She must have found them."

"But, Damascus will be gone soon. So she would rather die than move to a Sanctuary City?"

The driver sighs, as if preparing to address an indignant child. He says, "She would rather die where she belongs. If we went to the Sanctuary City, we would have no one. No comfort, no belonging. There is no dignity in spending the rest of your life in a place that is not for you."

"That's what you did, didn't you?"

"No. I stayed here."

The passenger processes this. She looks down at her unfolded map for the first time. The Submerged is close, but they first must pass through the buffer zone, a deserted world not yet reclaimed by ocean. Long gone are the days of uncharted lands. The scene, slipping by, is only lightly littered with past lives. The skeletons of homes and automobiles, and whatever else was not banished to undersea landfills or repurposed for Sanctuary construction.

"What do you mean, *here?* You live in the Submerged? That's impossible."

"With the taxi I can move around, from home to home. Sometimes I stay in the car. It's easy to avoid the field workers, you know, the patrollers. No one pays attention to taxis and tourists any more. Sanctuary 8 is not even one hundred miles away. I go pick up a customer, I get supplies, fill my tank, spare tires and fuel, any equipment I need is in my trunk."

"What happens when the Submerged expands? It can happen at any moment. You should have a permanent residence ready just in case."

"I don't have much longer to live. Let the sea take me."

There's a lot to uncover here. Nearly twenty million acres spread along a 1500 kilometer-long coastline, and countless homes, landmarks, and businesses flooded thousands of times over. My comments have been flooded lately by Sanctuary residents sharing stories about their visits to the Submerged to pay homage to their ancestors. I was lucky enough to be born in one of the Originals, in the heartland of America. There is so much history here, but I have always wanted to see where my grandparents were born. That is why I am here on the Pacific shore for my first venture into the Submerged West. Click through for photos and my top tips for getting here, camping out, and staying safe while checking out all the historic attractions still standing.

"When did you decide to move to the Sanctuary?"

"I didn't decide. I was a kid."

"Your parents must be Americans, then."

"No. Jerusalemites."

"Ah! Yes, the southern Quarter had plenty of Jerusalemites. I have never met one who was not born there."

A sting rises to the passenger's cheeks. She wants to tell him that no, she never saw Jerusalem, but she knew it like the back of her hand. It was painted on the walls of their family business, it was in the smell of the sesame-coated ka'ak they baked every morning for their customers. Sometimes her parents' memories mix in with her own, and she forgets that she had never held her mother's sweaty hand in the Mediterranean heat while walking through the Old City souq. This is hard to explain. She would try if she still had fluency in the language of the Quarter, that new Arab-ish the driver must know well, but it stayed in the Submerged like everything else.

Tip #1 – Since personal automobiles are still lawful in the Originals, there are many people who are still willing to drive Sanctuary residents out into the Submerged – for a price. If you don't live in the outermost territories, you'll need to shuttle-hop until you're somewhere near Sanctuaries 37-40 in the westernmost states before you reach the restricted zone. From there, you have the option of booking a rideshare or a solo cab. Apps specifically for Submerged tourism are abundant. I recommend Sub Trekker and Deep Desert Tours for the most highly-vetted and experienced drivers who can safely navigate the hinterland. You may need to arrange to switch drivers every hundred miles or so – there are no hydrogen fueling stations in the Submerged – but your efforts will pay off. These taxis are essential for recreating the experiences of decades past.

"It's here," the passenger says.

The taxi rolls to a stop. The driver angles the car towards the curb but stays several meters away from an overflow of water that has reached the road. This street meets the shoreline, despite miles of skyscrapers still extending west. Some emerge from the surface water perfectly intact, while others are worn from decades of acidic water lapping up against their outer walls.

The passenger can see the end of the ocean through a cleft in the cityscape. She rotates her neck in search of any memory triggers to give her a sense of home, but she can't. She is a tourist.

"Be careful. Don't touch the water."

The driver has taken his keys out of the engine and is standing outside of the taxi as well.

"I have to. I'm going in."

She unrolls a jumpsuit from her backpack and starts to slip it on. It is footed in order to seal out the water from any entryways to her skin. When all of her limbs are encased in the plasticky material, she shoves her hands into tight rubber gloves that snap-seal into place on her forearms.

The driver observes, his face a mix of concern and bewilderment. She wonders if he is surprised at her preparedness, at her intent on encroaching on the shore face.

He must have brought many reckless wanderers to this Submerged who know nothing about the acid waves and how tides change the land's shape, the skyline silhouette. Maybe he had tried to explore the Submerged Quarter himself and did not like what he saw.

She lifts her head toward the unchanged sky. When she was young, there was much talk of the birds dwindling overhead, but they endured too. They made habitats far from here, migrated to the sanctuaries meant for humans. Her mother always said they would outlast everything. They persisted from a time before the continents shrunk, before humans and all the animals that came before.

"The next high tide will be in three hours," the driver says before adding, half-joking, "Don't forget to come back."

The Arab Quarter's Great Revival
By George East

When World War I and the dismantling of the Ottoman Empire brought on a great migration of Arabs to America, Lower Manhattan became the site for a cultural renaissance. What we know as Little Syria is a misnomer however, as the transplants from Greater Syria did not only represent Syrian Arabs. Lebanese, Iraqi, Palestinians, and others came into the mix and brought aspects of home with them. Little Syria's vibrancy was short-lived, torn down to make way for the Brooklyn-Battery tunnel – but it's newly revived.

Now, the Washington Street and Battery Park area is more aptly named, with droves of Arabic speaking communities from all over Southwest Asia and North Africa filling in the gaps left by the recent flight of NYC-ers getting a head start on their new lives, far from the sinking coastline. The Arab world is shrinking much faster than the North-eastern United States, and it's certainly more densely populated with refugees

and asylum seekers than any other region. Tired of joining his-
torical camps for the stateless, new Arab Americans are eager to
start anew wherever they are given the space.

Thus, a shrine to Arab past and future is carved out in this
emptied Manhattan. The lands they yearn to recreate may be
long gone, some are covered in rubble and fire, some filled up with
saltwater. That doesn't stop those hungry for a homeland now
swallow up the depopulated pockets of Manhattan. A trio of oud
players host an impromptu concert on one side of Battery Park,
while a woman sells traditionally embroidered tunics on the oth-
er. Abandoned restaurants, once known for high-priced America-
na fare, now churn out plates of kibbeh and qatayef. This is the
Arab Quarter; come visit while it lasts. (continues on page B6)

With the map rolled in her fist, she drags her feet further into the Submerged.

The water feels cold through her boots and she is grateful the sun is so strong on her back. The outline of her shadow, sharpened by the contrast of bright and black, stretches out along the last dry patch of sidewalk and watches the tourist descend into the knee-deep. After some time, her waterproof suit, at first stiff and crackling around her limbs, softens to her body.

Had there been more travellers here, the tourist would have seen them wearing identical attire, fitted with the same branding as the knapsack sitting low and tight across her back. The Canadian sportswear company came highly recommended on a popular blog that chronicled one man's travels to every mile of Submerged in the U.S. down the western shoreline.

A hookah bar around the corner comes into view. The men who lounged outside the storefront and smoked green apple argileh are long gone by now. The tourist unzips her breast pocket and takes out her phone for a photo.

When her parents brought her there, the city was newly completed and droves of international sanctuary-seekers surged to it, hoping their presence would pull them off the waiting list limbo and into a permanent home. The U.S.-born filled up any space available in the Original states, also capping out the first eleven brand Sanctuary cities in the span of a decade.

They left New York City in the flood, and she couldn't stop thinking about all of her things drowning as they crossed into an oddly clean and organized Sanctuary.

The homes and apartment complexes on her new street were identical. The shrubs that divided the residential neighborhoods from the business districts were neatly squared off. Tiny plots of soil dotted the curb and from them pink begonias that encircled young trees. Freshly painted signs were everywhere, labelling every corner of the world with its exact purpose. When the tourist started school, she was greeted by volunteers from the Original States who, assuming she was not U.S.-born, would congratulate her on her English while correcting her accent.

Article 1

As predictive models prognose rapid rises in sea level and coastal land subsidence in the immediate future, and the impact of such phenomena along the urbanized coasts of every populated continent on Earth will displace at least 3 billion individuals, all Parties are to plan for the ethical relocation of the displaced, with the following goals in mind:

a.   Creating nationally defined sanctuary zones for the internally displaced and global refugees either by making space in existing residential areas or by developing new residential areas where land is currently unused.

a.   Reducing poverty and socio-political tensions from

intra- and international migration through economic stimu-
lation packages; mobilization of a federal workforce aimed at
expanding sanctuary zones; public assistance programs that
also encompass the domestic population; and other nationally
determined methods of social welfare.

(c)   Ensuring sanctuary zones do not significantly harm
wildlife, including endangered and non-endangered plant and
animal species, with special attention to conservation areas,
heritage districts, indigenous reservations, and other protected
lands.

The tourist moves along what must have been the Yemeni neighborhood on the western edge of the Arab Quarter but she cannot be certain. There is not enough time to go south and seek out the old apartment. She wants to photograph the sea-green carpet covered in the tracks her knuckles made when she dragged them across islands of pillows and Tupperware, the Styrofoam cups that she filled with plastic doll people and then knocked them all down, the bathtub in which her mother pushed her out into New York City noise, the slashed vinyl bar stools where she sat eating cereal on the last night, during the last argument her parents had about staying.

She tries to force herself to take it all in, but the labour of movement so far into the Submerged rips all the sentimentality out of her. The water seems to be congealing the longer she walks, sloshing at her hips. With little resistance, the tourist's gaze drops from the formidable miles of landscape in all directions to just the few meters of sea directly in front of her. Debris drifts into this narrowed scope of her vision as quickly as it bobs out. Golden splashes of late afternoon fall over the Submerged, dimming and brightening with the passing of clouds. The tourist concentrates on the shadows of every facade as they shapeshift around her. This distraction eases each strenuous step.

(continued from front page)

Under the American Preservation Act, new settlers of the Arab Quarter are unable to have permanent residence in the Original states once they are re-zoned to exclude the coastal restricted zones and the new Sanctuary zones. However, many internationals have come to these depopulated coastal states in order to be eligible for a waiting list of people seeking placement in the Sanctuary Cities, the first of which is slated to be completed in less than a decade. Even though U.S. citizens have priority, some native New Yorkers still plan to stay until the eleventh hour.

"Everyone who abandoned New York had somewhere else to go," says Marie Khan, a fifth-generation Manhattanite who refuses to make relocation plans. "They can talk about sea levels all they want. I'm staying put until I see the city sink."

Under the Honolulu Conventions, the U.S. has pledged 5 million nationally determined receptions (NDRs) and to build 40 Sanctuary Zones over 50 years. Some NDRs, mainly from the Southeast Asian Submerged, have been accepted early to join the Sanctuary City construction efforts after their cities flooded irreparably. Others, like Wafaa Ghudayya, were not fleeing flood when they arrived. Wafaa was recently married and pregnant in Jerusalem last year, when she was removed from her home under new national citizenship prioritization laws, aimed at making inland space for dwellers of the Mediterranean coast. Wafaa's husband, Ghassan, is the last owner of the centuries-old Jerusalem bakery, which will be soon demolished to make space for apartments and town homes overlooking the Holy City.

"I knew if we went to the camps with everyone else, we would have no livelihood. It would not be a safe place for my

wife to give birth. But here, we could keep our livelihood. I can keep making bread for our community."

The couple learned about the Arab Quarter from a relative, who had quick success opening a children's clothing store after rental fees plummeted due to mass exodus. They quickly made arrangements to arrive before Wafaa's due date. Word soon spread of the baker's arrival, along with the promise of Jerusalem-style ka'ak in New York. Their business is booming, their newborn healthy, Wafaa Ghudayya wishes for one more thing in her new life.

"I never want my child to forget where she comes from. We have built this new life to commemorate our land, to show people that we had a history and a home before this one."

She is surprised to find the front windows still intact. In the glass, she can see how the pockmarks in her skin catch the light and she flinches away from her reflection.

The blue awning is no longer there and the cafe is otherwise unmarked, but this is New Jerusalem. She walks around to the side of the building and finds the turquoise mosaic of the Jerusalem panorama fixed to the wall. Some of the tiles have fallen off, but the image is clear. She takes a photo.

There is a side window with a ledge that is a comfortable half-meter above the ocean surface. The tourist wades down the street to pull a loose brick from a nearby building. When she returns, it takes all of her energy to propel it through the glass. It fails to shatter on the first throw, and she has to use her boot to scoop the brick off the ground and into her hand underwater for a second attempt. This time, now that it has been compromised by a healthy spider crack, a large jagged opening forms. The tourist hoists herself up, thankful for all the exercising she had done in the weeks before this trip, and for the travel journalists who advised such preparations. She takes great care not to cut herself or her protective suit, as she swings her legs around and clumsily slides over the sill.

Her landing disturbs a dust blanket on the floor. She stands back up in a thick cloud reeking of mold. The undisturbed exterior of the cafe belies the blight inside. Charcoal grime plasters every surface, suppressing all the color. The ceiling appears chewed out, burst pipes peeking out through the gaps, dripping liquid into modest pools on the floor.

Everything is wet, even the air.

There isn't much time. The tourist sets to, but every few moments she dissociates from the task at hand. Every object she sees sparks a new memory she did not know she once possessed, but she can't take it all with her. Each bistro set has a circular table covered in geometric shapes. They look hand painted, but the tourist does not know who from the neighborhood would have done the decoration. There is almost no one left to ask.

She whips off her knapsack and fishes out a rag. She rubs at the table to get the grime off, before she realizes she's erasing some of the paint as well. In a panic, she runs to the next bistro set and cleans the table more delicately, streaming drops of water from her canteen to help loosen the dried sludge. That is good enough. With the flash on her camera phone she captures the table. She walks around the pastry display case, cleans and captures the antique espresso machine. Majestic and brass, her mother refused to have it removed when they rented the space.

She turns and captures the canvas rice bags nestled along all the window sills. They once served as back cushions. Then she captures the exposed pipes and the broken window and the empty, blackened pastry case.

The light shifts and time is real again. The tourist pulls a chair to the window. The water is several inches closer to the ledge now.

"Shit," she whispers.

There are about a dozen frames on the wall, evenly spaced like a gallery grid. It would be a waste of time to try and clean off every single one to see what they hold.

The tourist settles on taking the bottom of her canteen to the glazing, one by one, and smashes out the glass. It hurts to see the frames her mother had carefully selected for the New Jerusalem aesthetic to be yanked from their chosen places and strewn on the floor.

She takes care not to tear the photo of her parents in front of the cafe on opening day. She places it in the silicone freezer bag, along with the only photos of her as a baby that exist. Her father grins in the next frame, as a boy, grinning in the old Jerusalem bakery alongside his father and his father's father. Her mother looking studious in a university library in Beirut, Submerged, goes into the freezer bag too. Finally, she folds up the article about her parents in Battery Gazette, the last print-only newspaper in the Original States.

With these artifacts stacked and zipped in silicone freezer bags, she reaches behind the counter for the last of the remains. They are still there, the stacks of notepads on which her father did his accounting the old-fashioned way. She will never be able to decipher his strange system, but she will have his handwriting.

Tip # 2 – Plan to get to your destination early at low tide. You don't want to be any more than waist-deep in the ocean, as the nearshore zone is a toxic mix of water and waste, and highly acidic. And depending on the time and place, if you are too far into the Submerged at high tide, the turbulent waters could be fatal. Don't take the risk.

The driver had put the car in reverse and retreated from the encroaching waves as they pushed back the hinterland. He watched the waves and the digital clock on the dashboard and the descending sun at the same time. He has driven many people to the Submerged city in his life, hundreds, and he has never waited on the eastern edge for one of them to drown until now.

When the waves darken and the light goes coral, her silhouette appears faintly like a mirage. The driver must have missed her body swimming from a distance, her body just a shadow in a sea of shadows. The closer she gets, the more clear his wild eyes become.

He is fearful for her, and of her, his body leaning out of the driver's seat.

He had just convinced himself that this woman came to the Submerged to die, and now he was seeing her ghostly emergence from the water. His passenger might have laughed at his stupor if she wasn't in such shock herself. When she is near, he is unable to berate her.

"We need to go quickly."

The passenger is already peeling the jumpsuit off and prepares to toss it in the back seat. This motion seems to have shaken him awake.

"You have to leave that here."

She hesitates. It's a silly thing, the ingrained fear of littering in the Submerged.

She knows the contaminated suit belongs here, in lawless land. She will go back to the Sanctuary Cities, those shiny new things that are worth trying to preserve and protect, not yet burial grounds covered in gray and sour sky.

The driver presses. "We have to go now."

Part of her wanted to stay here too, join the driver in his delusion that this could still be a home. Of course, they were nothing to each other but reminders of a could-have-been and a what-was-once.

Instead of the white high beams blasting out all of his color, it could have been the glow of a streetlamp on his face on a busy street. A street vendor's cart could have spit hot oil at them as the seller fished out sizzling balls of deep fried dough. They could have bought a whole plate of them doused in syrup for just a few dollars and walked absently into city noise.

Her mind returns to the present, to the sopping gear in her gloved hand.

"I just don't want to leave it here," she says.

They could have done all those things if things were different, but they weren't, and now there is no return. But the passenger and the driver each have footprints out there in the deep, and that has to be enough.

He seems to follow her thoughts. He speaks softer this time, telling her, "We left everything else."

Exhibit K

By Nadia Afifi

Nadia Afifi lives in the U.S., but grew up in the Kingdom of Bahrain in the Persian Gulf, where she watched the archipelago nation modernize and transform itself. She tells us that this science fiction story was inspired in part by imagining the home of her childhood in a hopeful light, with both its complicated past and a thriving future. Her first novel The Sentient *was released in September 2020.*

The dead woman opened her eyes to a veil of light. She blinked several times, focusing on the sand-colored surface only inches from her face. Walls surrounded her from all sides, a narrow, glowing tomb.

She peered down over her chin, noting exposed breasts, followed by the hills of her knees, slightly bent. Her mouth felt dry, her head heavy. A trio of dark lines ran across her upper-right arm, a tattoo she had no recollection of getting.

Her neck itched, but when she reached up to scratch it, her arms remained at her sides. Similar attempts to move her legs, feet, toes proved equally fruitless – she was immobile except for her head. Her breath quickened, the first stages of panic setting in.

Before she could test her lungs, a voice cut through the silence.

"Please remain calm." The disembodied voice was female, reassuring. "Do not struggle, and you will be released shortly."

The frozen woman did not know her own name or how she came to be there, but whoever she was, she distrusted voices without an owner, promises conjured from air. Panic choked her, burning her throat. She rammed her head, the only part of her she could move, from side to side.

In the throes of panic, a memory surfaced. She had been trapped in the center of a crowd, pushed and jostled in every direction. The stream of bodies passed through a gap in a wall crowned with barbed wire, the sky thick with smoke. A voice rang in her ear, a distant warning. *Don't turn around. Keep moving.* She strained to look back in the voice's direction, but the crowd pressed forward in a current of fear and sweat, carrying her away. She screamed.

"Please remain calm," the voice repeated, and a needle emerged from the side of the chamber, advancing towards her neck. Its bite was sharp.

She awoke strapped to a chair. Cold air filled her nostrils, the sterile smell of a hospital ward. Shapes darted around her, faster than her eyes could focus. Voices followed, speaking in garbled English. Her body tensed. Her relief at regaining motion was tempered by the fact that she remained bound by unknown captors. A white dressing gown, soft like sand, covered her thighs.

Her hand moved reflexively to her side, closing around something sharp. A syringe, which she gripped with practised confidence. The weapon triggered a new memory, of a foggy marsh where grass reached her neck. A rifle hung across her shoulders, its wooden handle etched with signatures, imprints of forgotten names. At some point in the past, she had fought. Had she killed?

She found her first target, an old man in a lab coat, standing across the room. Their eyes met and the man's mouth twitched in an intimate, conspiratorial smile she did not return. Though dizzy, she leaned forward, tubes tugging at her wrists.

Another burst of light flooded her senses. The wall behind the man opened, parting to reveal an applauding audience.

The old man turned to her with a broad smile.

"Ladies and gentlefolk, give warm greetings to Lt. Selma Carmichael!"

The crowd cheered. Her hand loosened its grip, the syringe clattering to the ground.

Behind her, a screen flashed, displaying a montage of news footage and still images. Music swelled from every direction, blasting a soaring, triumphant melody. At the center, the words "Exhibit K: Voices from the Past" appeared.

The applause died down. A light shone on the center of the hospital room, now a stage.

Her head ached. The woman suddenly realized that a strange, glowing device had been secured around her neck. A staff member fastened her wrists to the chair, capitalizing on her shock. An orange substance snaked down the clear tube, burning as it found her vein. She jerked back angrily, but her hands remained bound to the armrests.

Selma – assuming that was her real name – scanned the audience for a familiar face, an anchor in her mental fog, but only found strangers, faces alight with matched fascination. Several eyes lit up in the dark like the flash of a camera bulb.

Who are these people? she thought. The crowd stared at her hungrily, the air thick with anticipation while she struggled against her bindings.

The old man leaned forward with a sympathetic expression. The music faded.

"As you can see, ladies and gentlefolk, it's a jarring experience for those who awaken," he said in a clear, booming voice. "They come out of freezing with limited physical and cognitive functioning. Part of the joy of the Exhibit Series, nonetheless, is seeing our heroic subjects remember who they were, and discover what lies ahead."

Know your terrain. The phrase came to Selma in a chiding voice, an old lesson with new meaning. Understand the battlefield before the first strike.

As a thousand eyes stared and the orange liquid warmed her temples, Selma took a deep breath and pieced threads of information together. Her name was Lt. Selma Carmichael. *The first name, she was born with, the last name acquired, the title earned.* She had said that to someone long ago; she could even recall the appreciative laughter that followed. She had fought in a war. Now she sat strapped to a chair, an object of fascination on a stage. Was she a prisoner?

"Where am I?" she asked, her voice hoarse. The old man turned to her, surprised, and the crowd hummed excitedly.

"As I stated before, your name is Lt. Selma Carmichael," the man said. "You died of cancer in the year 2108, after consenting to be placed in a cryonic state. My name is Dr. Hugh, and I successfully revived you today. It is now 2354, and much has happened in between. Welcome back."

The room spun. She closed her eyes, the ensuing applause drowned by the pounding in her ears.

The man's words, perhaps combined with the device pulsing against her head, unleashed memories, slivers of time and moments and people she loved. A life, in its entirety.

She had left Turkey during the first wave of droughts, before the border closed. At a checkpoint, one of the militias pulled her father aside, forcing him to sit with a group of male prisoners. He had told her not to look back, even as she struggled against the crowd. Whether he was recruited into a militia, tortured or killed, Selma never learned. In that first year in the Camp from Hell, she lost herself in the world of dark potentials, imagining how her father died, how much pain and fear he felt in his final moments. She didn't have to imagine her mother's death, spending a week wiping back sweat and vomit and shit until her mother succumbed to dysentery.

Not until the People's Army came did Selma abandon the past and learn to live again. From that point on, she fought for the displaced, for clean water, land and safety, all the things she once took for granted.

She remembered dying. Her end came slowly, not in a remote jungle battleground but an outpatient clinic in Mecca, California, a man at her side. She remembered the top of his head resting on the foot of the bed. His presence had comforted her but also weighed her down, making her feel complicit somehow, sharing her pain without weakening its power. She had searched for words of comfort, some witty comment to show that it was alright, she was ready, but found nothing to say. Outside the window, the sky had been bright and cloudless, a single Joshua tree visible behind the parking lot. The truck arrived early in preparation, the words "Anubis Cryonics" slanted across its side. She was thirty-seven.

"Who are these people?" she asked. "Why am I here?"

"You paid for a second chance, and you got one," Dr. Hugh said with a smile. "And you are special. We don't revive everyone, for assorted reasons. But there was no question that you deserved another chance at life, and in the process, we will help you understand your old one."

She looked down at her body again, strong and healthy, without the sallow hue and jutting bones that marked her final months in the outpatient clinic.

"The body is on permanent loan to you," he said, as though reading her mind. "You only came to us with your lovely head. We attached the rest. You may have noticed an itch in your neck, which I assure will pass soon."

Selma wondered if Dr. Hugh could in fact read her mind, but decided not to ask. She did not wish to know the body's origins. The skin tone perfectly matched her own, the color of clouded coffee. Her stomach knotted painfully.

The show continued. Selma followed her own life summary on the screen, while Dr. Hugh narrated.

"Welcome to another series of "History Reborn," where the past comes to life," Dr. Hugh announced. Subtitles ran across the screen. "As you'll be aware from the previews, Exhibit K will focus on the infamous Climate Wars, a time of upheaval when seas rose and nations fell. In our interactive immersion, you'll meet the key players of the conflict, ask them the questions we all want to know the answers to, and best of all, experience a first-hand, all-senses recreation of one of the most seminal battles of the war – the Battle of Three Rivers."

"Our heroine – born Selma Kavak in a humble Turkish village – became an iconic symbol of those displaced in the Climate Wars when a photograph of her went viral in 2097, days before the Battle of Three Rivers."

And there she was, smiling back from the screen. Selma had endured years of combat by the time that image was taken, but her face retained a youthful energy, her eyes shining despite days without sleep. She wore her hair in a long side braid, looking over her shoulder at the camera. Her olive-green shirt left her arms exposed, revealing a fresh tattoo of three vertical lines (which, Selma realized with a glance at her arm, someone must have applied to her new body), along with a hint of cleavage – undoubtedly a factor in the image's immediate popularity. At the time, women in combat remained a novelty in her part of the world.

Ignoring the audience and Dr. Hugh, Selma stared at her younger self, separated by time and death and all that she didn't yet know. In that moment over two centuries ago, Selma had been ready to die. So many had gone before her, she had not expected to survive the war. But still, she smiled, because she was alive at that moment and had so many, living and dead, to fight for.

Instead, Selma survived. She had met Connor, her eventual widower, after the war. He came from a temperate place with rolling, green hills, unscathed by conflict (at least in that century), and he might as well have been a mythical creature from a parallel world. *Sheltered*, she pronounced him when they met, with equal parts envy and wonder, that they walked the Earth at the same time but experienced it so differently. She wanted to resent him, but it was hard to begrudge a good person a good life. They retreated to the California desert, which resembled the world as it should be – quiet, free, unmolested.

Five years later, Selma began coughing up blood. Lung cancer, a doctor in Loma Linda pronounced, no doubt caused by inhaling several lifetimes of chemical weapons during the Climate Wars. She sat in silence on the drive home, watching the sun dissolve into the mountains and wondering how many sunsets she had left. For the first time, she feared death – truly feared it, beyond animal adrenaline. More accurately, she feared losing her happiness just when she found it. She feared never experiencing the future so many had sacrificed for.

Selma had never believed the clergymen of her childhood in Turkey, the monks of Asia or the corporate shamans of the west, all promising a life beyond life. She had seen enough death to accept its finality, but perhaps science, stronger than ever after the Climate Wars, could provide a loophole in nature's contract. They had sat together in Anubis Cryonics' Los Angeles office, she and Connor, holding hands under the table. Her wrists were already weak by that point, but she signed the requisite forms, relinquishing her head and one fourth of her neck to a freezing facility in Tempe, Arizona. A final, desperate hope for a second chance.

Connor. Selma tore away from the screen back to Dr. Hugh, who was now taking questions from the audience.

"Where's my husband?" she asked, her voice clearer than before. "Was he revived?"

Dr. Hugh nodded subtly to the camera, as if the interruption had been planned.

"Selma, we will tell you everything in a more private setting," he said. "Trust me, you would prefer that. But before we end the opener, we have another character from the Climate Wars to welcome back to life."

Another wall parted, revealing a middle-aged man slumped in a similar chair. His mouth hung slightly open as his head lolled to one side, his blue eyes vacant. An attendant pushed him closer, revealing a distinct crew cut and blunt features. Selma gasped. Dr. Hugh nodded approvingly.

"Our heroine's antagonist is Martin Axelrod," he said with a flourish, while the audience dutifully hissed. "The infamous CEO of Atlas Enterprises, the conglomerate responsible for the industrial overexpansion that fuelled the Climate Wars, and which later provided the mercenary units that fought for Industry in the Asian and South American arenas."

A familiar current of anger ran through Selma's tiring limbs. Axelrod hid in Atlas headquarters in Laos at the time of the Three Rivers battle. Despite her best efforts, she failed to kill him. He retreated to China at the war's end, outliving her and countless others.

And there he sat, though he gave no recognition of an enemy only feet away. A dense glob of saliva leaked from the corner of his mouth. Martin Axelrod had not revived as successfully as Selma, Dr. Hugh conceded, but he vowed that Axelrod would improve enough to answer for his crimes. With that final remark, he bowed before the applauding audience and the walls closed in.

The Exhibit K production team placed Selma in her own room, which they assured her was not a prison, although she must remain there for her own safety. The world had changed beyond her comprehension in the last century, they warned, and she would not function well outside of the exhibit's walls. She understood them when they spoke to her, but their own conversations were harder to follow, though not impossible – she assumed that the staff had learned the dialect from her own time to communicate effectively. The Exhibit show itself had also been comprehensible, perhaps a courtesy for her.

The room could only be described as minimalist, with bare walls, a matching desk and bookshelf, a clean bed and a corner filled with exercise equipment. Connor used to tease her about her hatred of exercise, before reassuring her that she never needed it. He would wake up before dawn to run, evading the desert heat. A staff member gestured her towards a small platform suspended inches above the floor – a treadmill.

She searched for a means of escape that first night. Her room was large but confined, the only open side walled with a dense, glass-like substance, which resisted all her attempts to break through. The glass wall revealed a long hallway with adjacent rooms, where Selma assumed Axelrod also waited.

A single, narrow slit of a window sat ten feet high on the back wall, the only source of natural light in the room.

It was night – stars blinked through the cloudy sky, but the opening did not reveal any buildings or clues to her location. She dragged a chair underneath it, preparing to jump up.

"Are you planning to shrink to the size of a mouse and squeeze through?" a voice inquired behind her.

Dr. Hugh stood on the other side of the glass wall, hands folded behind his back. He gestured politely at a chair. Instead, Selma walked to the glass, meeting his calm, grey eyes.

"I'll keep trying until I get answers," she said. "What is this place and where's my husband?"

"Connor Carmichael has not yet been revived," Dr. Hugh said. "Unfortunately, the process to unfreeze someone from your era is not a simple one. We need to get the right permissions."

"What do you mean the right –?" Selma began, but Dr. Hugh raised his hand in a gesture of surrender.

"I realize that he was the reason you underwent the procedure in the first place," he said in a kind voice that did nothing to stop Selma's heart from pounding. "And if you are cooperative and demonstrate an ability to adapt, I will do everything in my power to make it happen. But you must understand – you come from a more primitive time, and many are reluctant to open the floodgates to everyone who wanted to live again."

"It's wrong," Selma said. "We signed a contract."

"Think about it this way, my dear – if you could bring back people from Medieval times, when wars were as common as rain and people were burned alive for interpreting the Bible differently – would you want those people walking among you? Would they even be able to cope in modern times, with electricity and free thinking?"

"I'd like to talk to some of them," Selma countered. "Da Vinci, Copernicus."

"Exactly! The famous, the movers and shakers, those who mattered. That is the entire purpose of the Exhibit series. Though you never planned to be, Selma, you mattered. You were the right person at the right time. Sadly, your husband did not make the history books, which makes his case harder."

Selma lay awake all night. Dr. Hugh, and presumably others like him, deemed the Climate Wars era as primitive and dangerous. She couldn't disagree, but from what she had seen, had humanity really improved in 2354? She had awoken to a society that turned her and others into zoological exhibits, complete with glass cages. Her husband was deemed unworthy of a second life, yet Martin Axelrod, a war criminal, lay drooling somewhere within the Exhibit walls.

The right person at the right time. What had Selma done that was more important, more significant, than others in the war? She was not special. She was famous for a picture.

Selma feared sleep, even more so after her death. In the past, sleep marked the time when she was most vulnerable to ambush and capture. Now, sleep had become a temporary return to nothingness. The time between her passing in California to waking up in the chamber elapsed without a tunnel of light or an afterlife, but it also had not been completely instantaneous. She recalled a slow, elastic stretch of time – not two hundred years-worth, but a sense of sinking backwards into peaceful darkness. The experience frightened her more than if no time had passed at all, if she had simply blinked and come alive again.

The tattoo on her right arm, so carefully replicated, commemorated the three weeks she spent lost in Cambodia, separated from her company. She had travelled by night and slept under dense branches during the day, evading predators in all forms. Wounded in a skirmish and dizzy with dehydration, she eventually found herself in fields of tiger grass, a plant known for its healing properties, which she placed over her many injuries. When she reached the outskirts of Phnom Penh, rested and reunited with her unit, she found a tattoo parlor and had three blades of grass inked onto her arm.

Against all odds, she had survived. She cheated death until the very end, and then cheated it again by being regenerated in this strange place, where she'd never felt more helpless or alone.

Selma found a routine in the following weeks. An hour on the treadmill before breakfast, followed by weights and another hour of reading classic novels from the bookshelf. Connor would be proud.

After lunch, Selma sat in her glass prison while visitors to the Exhibit passed by. Some simply stared at her, whispering amongst themselves and taking pictures, while others questioned her in their garbled, fractured version of English. She responded with silence. A few greeted her in Turkish, prompting flickers of a smile. The smiles were rare – Selma veered between periods of frustration and heavy sadness, a fog that sapped her will to eat, speak or show interest in the endless stream of intruders.

Dr. Hugh assessed her at the end of each day, asking about her memory and overall well-being, but continued to evade the topic of Connor's revival. Cooperate, he reassured her, and I'll fight to make it happen. Selma complied in the hope that the alleged doctor would keep his promise. Without it, she would exist in limbo, everyone she had ever cared for long dead.

Others came to visit Selma with more specific purpose. Academics, historians, reporters interested in the Climate Wars, to confirm facts or gain new insight. A pair of college students, who shared the easy familiarity of a couple, scheduled frequent, private interviews to learn about Selma's life before and after the war.

"What was it like to live in houses without SP – without smart programming?" the young woman asked her during their first interview. She reminded Selma of an exotic doll, with her delicate features, dyed silver hair and henna that ran up her arms.

"It was just the way it was," Selma said, recalling how her grandmother used to say similar things before a bus explosion scattered her across the streets of Ankara. "If we were cold, we tried to make ourselves warm. If we needed light, we turned it on ourselves, or used flashlights and candles when the electricity gave out, which happened frequently during the war."

They took feverish notes without looking down, their thoughts transcribing on thin tablets. They had many conveniences in this strange future – "smart rooms" that adjusted light, temperature and appliances to a person's mental command, virtual sports leagues, fantasy simulations and classrooms. Meeting Selma in person, they told her, was a rare treat outside of virtual reality, a fact confirmed by their pallid complexions, white like old bones.

"Tell me more about the Asteroid Belt colony," Selma said, recalling a snippet of conversation from their last meeting. "How big are the stations? What are they shaped like?"

The man smiled cautiously. Undoubtedly coached by Dr. Hugh, they hesitated at describing too much of the world beyond the Exhibit walls, but Selma encouraged them with a rare smile.

"They're circular, to support internal gravity, but only carry around 100,000 people each," the man said. Though halting, he spoke in perfect archaic English, as they referred to Selma's speech. "It's rustic living, more so than Mars and Luna. Probably closer to life in your time."

Instead of taking notes, Selma sketched as they talked. Elaborate stations, round domes on faraway planets, a world (or more accurately, worlds) that once seemed impossible. After the couple left, she would add herself and Connor to the drawings. During lulls between battles, Selma had always sketched her surroundings, no matter how terrible the landscape. Drawing it made everything permanent somehow, in a place where nothing and no one lasted long.

Selma thanked them, providing more details about showering in unregulated water. They followed this pattern each meeting, exchanging knowledge that left both parties satisfied. From an early age, Selma learned that life was a series of transactions, some fairer than others.

"Capitalistic, neo-liberal drivel," Connor used to tell her when she spoke that way. "Not everything's a transaction. You and I are not a transaction."

Connor had always tried to lure Selma into political debates, which she humored for a brief time before ceding defeat. The Climate Wars had ended, the struggle of her lifetime won. What else was there to argue about?

The meetings gave Selma temporary relief from her lapses into despair, but Connor's absence gnawed at her like a constant hunger. She stared at her drawings, tempted by the idea of escape to those remote places where she might find a semblance of a life. But to leave would be to abandon Connor, whose buried consciousness Dr. Hugh dangled as bait. As the days progressed, however, the walls around her felt closer, her prison more and more like a second tomb. If she were to escape, she reasoned, it would be to find Connor, wherever they kept him, and find a way to demand his unfreezing. She had survived worse odds.

Several nights later, opportunity struck. Only one attendant brought her dinner, the other sick with flu. Selma dimmed the lights, feigning rest. She moved quietly, a small free weight in hand, while the attendant lowered the meal onto her table.

Focusing on the back of the man's head, Selma hesitated. There was no honor in attacking someone with their back turned, an unsuspecting civilian. Then again, an employee at Exhibit K was also a jailer, confining Selma and others against their will.

Selma brought the weight down in a swift motion. The man let out a soft gasp before crumpling to the floor. She checked for a pulse – faint, but regular. She found a badge in his pocket, swiped the door open and stepped outside.

Selma ran down the hallway, her bare feet light against the cool floor. She clutched the small weight, silently hoping there were no cameras overhead. She needed to be fast, and merciless if necessary.

The adjacent rooms bore the same size and structure to her own, filled with interactive exhibits of the Climate Wars – old battle footage, interviews with the Chinese president, and samples of "archaic" weapons. She glanced through each window as she ran down the hallway but didn't linger.

In the last exhibit room before the exit door, she found Martin Axelrod.

The mercenary had improved since his debut on the Exhibit stage, but not by much. His skin, already pale, had the appearance of melted wax. Even his hair seemed drained of color. He stared blankly ahead, muttering under his breath. Selma approached the window and his pale eyes widened with recognition. She turned on the speaker, as she had seen Dr. Hugh and countless others do.

"That's right," Selma whispered, anger swelling in her chest. "You remember me, don't you? We never met, but you knew my picture and what I said about you after the war. How my greatest regret was not killing you in Laos."

Selma looked down at the crude weapon in hand, her arm tensing with purpose. Without his imposing, trademark body armor and retinue of henchmen, Axelrod never looked more vulnerable than now, a lame animal begging to be put down. Through the glass, Axelrod eyed Selma's clenched fist, his face flickering with that old calculation.

"You thought you were better than me?" Axelrod asked. His voice croaked as hers had done. "You ecoterrorists would have flattened that city and anyone you suspected of collaborating with us. All for trees and flowers."

"For our lives," she retorted, voice rising until it echoed across the hushed corridor. "You can say what you like, but you fought for profit. You killed for the people destroying our world. Look around you – the history books chose the winning side."

Axelrod's laughter dissolved into a fit of coughing.

"Some future, isn't it?" he said between gasps. "I'd say neither side won in the end."

Before she could respond, light came on at the far end of the hallway and Selma's heart sank. She sprinted through the exit door.

Selma stumbled into the mezzanine level of an expansive, empty atrium. The shops and restaurants bordering the central walkway were boarded up for the evening, but an elaborate fountain continued to run in the center. At first, it appeared no different than a typical museum, until a burst of motion drew Selma's eyes upward.

An enormous screen covered the domed ceiling, relaying a montage of three-dimensional images, words, sounds with such staggering intensity, Selma had to steady herself against the railing. The unmistakable sights of a battle projected from the screen, bodies falling through crumbling debris and mud. The Siege of Istanbul. She was there.

An explosion struck a car in the upper-right section of the dome, and Selma felt the rush of heat against her skin, the smell of charred metal. This was her memory, on the screen, in all its hideous detail. Shocked, she inched slowly downstairs to the main floor, training her eyes on the ground.

Another flash of movement caught her eye and she spun around to face two guards. She raised the weight, still secure in her sweaty fist, but one of the men held a device of his own, a silver baton. A pulse emanated from its centre and a cold, numbing sensation spread from Selma's chest out to the rest of her body. She collapsed on the floor, a pair of boots blocking her way to the front door, before everything went dark.

Selma opened her eyes, the blurred outline of Dr. Hugh coming into focus across the room. For the first time, he sat on the same side of the glass wall, his face etched in dismay.

"You were doing so well," he said, ignoring Selma as she vomited over the side of the bed. "Participating in the Exhibit, educating people. They need educating. Everyone wants to look ahead, for the new gadget or the latest scandal. It's hard to make people see how far they've come. That's how you help, Selma, and make our world better."

"I don't care about your world," Selma said, pulling herself upright with a shudder. "I want a real life, with Connor. I want a family, a chance to start again. If I'd known I'd exist as an animal in a cage –"

Unable to finish the thought, Selma stood up and threw a chair against the glass wall. It bounced off harmlessly, the surface as smooth and unflinching as Dr. Hugh, who watched her without reaction.

"Life is always preferable to death," the old man said, a dark shadow passing over his face. "That is a value humanity has learned the hard way, although people of your time were different, happy to kill themselves for invisible gods and other intangibles. You are not the first in the Exhibit to express a desire to return to nothingness, even knowing that it is indeed nothing that awaits you. But why? Why not seize the opportunities we give you?"

"I did," Selma said with a bitter smile, nodding towards the far exit. Dr. Hugh shook his head and stood up.

"As a concession to you, I will have the interactive stage of our Exhibit moved ahead of schedule," he said. "It will give you a chance to get out of this room and remember who your real enemies are. You'll even get the chance to change the course of history, in a way. Believe it or not, Selma, I want to help you. I know your story better than anyone else living. Play your part well, and we'll honor our bargain to revive your husband."

Selma hesitated. The doctor wore many faces – showman, educator, therapist, overseer, reluctant ally – none of which she trusted. However, she had nothing left to lose. Either he would uphold his promise, or she would find a way to end her existence a second and final time.

She nodded.

"What do you mean interactive?" Selma asked as he opened the door.

"Did you not listen on opening day?" he asked with a thin smile. "We're going to war."

The Battle of the Three Rivers carried a deceptively dramatic name in the history books – there was only one major river, the Mekong, and two nearby tributaries, where the carnage unfolded. Axelrod's mercenaries and the Chinese army occupied Vientiane, while the Displaced People's Army attacked from the north and west.

The battle lasted nine days and ten nights, the longest recorded during the Climate Wars. With robotic infantry not yet adopted in Asia, combat was largely hand-to-hand, aided by tanks and electromagnetic weapons. Simple, brutal, human.

Selma joined the first wave crossing the Mekong. Atlas fighters defended their posts along the muddy banks of the city's outskirts, raining bullets and stunners onto the advancing riverboats. She jumped out with the rest of her unit before the boat reached the shore, deflecting and returning fire. The ground, drowning in days of rain, slid underneath her boots as her feet found land.

It all felt real – the smell of the river water, the rising smoke over the city. The explosions, the dense thud of bodies falling around her. The adrenaline, keeping her moving through devastation and death. Then a camera would flash along the shore, figures pointing and hands raising devices to record the scene. Some merely watched. Others had paid to be participants, although when shot, they simply fell to the ground, a red "X" spreading across their chests. They laughed as their game ended, helped each other up and followed Selma's advance into the city.

They had dressed her in the same outfit from her iconic picture, her hair braided to one side. Her new body was young and responsive, allowing her to leap and zigzag around huts and battered buildings with relative ease.

A bullet whistled past her ear, making her heart spasm. She spun around to find a team of fighters in Atlas uniform, human and virtual. Both looked identical, but when she unloaded her semi-automatic, some evaporated into air while others fell unharmed, marked with an "X."

A golden temple loomed several blocks away. The sunlight danced across its shining domes, a beacon through the smoke. Martin Axelrod had set up Atlas headquarters in a warehouse where children used to make tennis shoes. In the real battle, Selma never made it that far. An explosion had ripped through an intersection three blocks from the temple, and command summoned all troops to the east, to finish off the Chinese units.

In the end, they won, but Axelrod escaped before the People's Army took the airport. This time, Selma had no commands to obey.

Selma crossed the intersection before the explosion hit, dodging bullets and debris. The streets of Vientiane, recreated with astonishing detail, had become a game board in which she knew all the rules and plays in advance. She advanced with confidence and purpose. Either revenge and Connor awaited her, or the game was rigged to begin with, and her suffering would end.

The warehouse faced the temple, sun-bleached and lifeless in its shadow. No sign marked Atlas headquarters, but the formidable presence of masked gunmen told Selma she had found the right place. She gestured to a virtual soldier behind her, mouthing for a hand grenade – to her surprise, he obliged.

The grenade reached the entrance before the Atlas men could react, sending heat and flesh into the air before the limbs evaporated like hot steam. The survivors returned fire.

Selma jerked back, feeling a familiar burning sensation through her right arm. A trail of blood ran down her shoulder, over the tattooed blades of tiger grass.

Her suspicions confirmed, Selma almost laughed. *I'm playing by different rules,* she thought. *I can get hurt, and so can Axelrod.*

She ran across the street to an overturned car, firing along the way. Others in her unit joined the attack, taking down the remaining guards. The coast clear, she ran into the warehouse.

She found him on the third level. Axelrod's office overlooked the river, where the battle continued. A desk near the window was nearly invisible under layers of clutter, a small, sputtering fan scattering papers onto the floor. A radio perched on the windowsill played Christmas songs, even though it was June.

Behind the desk, Martin Axelrod faced the window. Selma spun his chair around, but he looked at her without seeing. His military fatigues emphasized strong shoulders and a fighter's body, but his face was lined and tired, like her own.

He held a small picture in his hand, a framed photo of a woman and small child. His head jerked in the direction of Selma's gun.

"Get it over with," he said.

Selma's fingers tightened around the gun, but she hesitated.

"Your family," she said. "They went into freezing, didn't they?"

Axelrod laughed bitterly, his cold blue eyes meeting hers directly, for the first and last time.

"You don't realize it yet," he said softly. "They won't revive them, our families. They thawed out the heads long ago. Incinerated them. I heard the guards, but I suspected it once I realized where I was. Contracts mean nothing to these people. There's only us left. So finish it, and there'll only be you."

Selma swayed where she stood. She opened her mouth to speak, but there was nothing else to be said. She knew it was true. Dr. Hugh had lied and would never revive Connor, just as Axelrod would not live beyond his purpose as a spectacle, a symbol of retroactive justice. Both were merely characters, walking like ghosts through a world that had ended long ago.

Selma bent over the desk, struggling for air. Others had joined them in the office, men and women in strange clothes, taking pictures through their hungry eyes and recording the scene on small devices. Several cameras lined the room, perhaps broadcasting the battle's climax on some distance stage. Selma imagined the walls parting again, the heat of the city giving way to an air-conditioned stadium, where Dr. Hugh would ask her how it felt, to kill an enemy at last.

She dropped the gun. The spectators closed in, circling and whispering together. A young man darted between Selma and Axelrod, posing for a picture.

Selma lurched forward, as though pushed by an invisible hand. She leaped across the desk in a single, almost graceful motion, and out through the open window. The radio played "Jingle Bells" through the alarmed screams and clamors of battle, and soft rain dusted her face as the ground drew near.

Selma opened her eyes, gasping as hideous, throbbing pain greeted her lower body. In front of her, her legs were lifted apart by straps, both encased in glowing casts. Blood pounded in her ears, an echo of the fall. After several deep breaths, she recognized the green-tinged lighting and sterile air of the medical ward, where she was first paraded before an audience.

Dr. Hugh sat to her right, free of his former warmth. Her pulse slowing, Selma sighed.

"We can eliminate the pain," Dr. Hugh said. "But you don't seem willing to accept our help, no matter how much we try."

"So you can send me back into that... circus?"

"It's the price, Selma," he said. "For being alive. Why did you jump?"

"Connor's dead," she said.

"For hundreds of years, Selma."

"You know what I mean," Selma said, noting the dullness in her voice. The pain felt reassuring as she spoke, affirming the cold ache in her chest. "He's gone for good. You never planned to revive him."

Dr. Hugh opened his mouth to speak, but retreated under Selma's gaze. He nodded.

"You can't have the life you once did," Dr. Hugh said, his gentle tone returning. "It's not the same world you left. But it is life all the same, and once you recover, you will go back to the Three Rivers, you will fight, and show the world why you deserve to be here. You will live."

"No more fighting," Selma said simply. "I won't be an actor in your sick theater, and if you place me there – "

"You will fight!" Dr. Hugh bellowed.

"I'll jump," she said. "And I'll jump again, each time at the end, until even you can't bring me back."

The museum hours closed at seven p.m., but the lights remained on in the Archive ward. Exhibit L had premiered the week before: an immersive, interactive display of the Robot and Non-Humanoid Rights Movement at the start of the twenty-second century.

Selma spent each day on the exhibit floor, posing for pictures and answering questions with a smile. It's true, the sea crept over coastal cities and heat killed the crops in the world's dry, poor places. No, I never regretted joining the People's Army. Yes, I'm grateful for each day.

Her uniform covered the hideous bruise along her side, but Dr. Hugh had removed the casts on both of her legs.

His anger over her jump, her refusal to play the game, waned when the ratings came in, along with the public outcry on Selma's behalf. The two college students had visited Selma during her recovery, sharing articles that praised Selma's statement as an act of resistance, a naming of her true enemy. Other commentators just enjoyed the unexpected twist in the battle.

The nights belonged to Selma. This was her bargain with Dr. Hugh. She returned to her ward each night, the glass doors swinging open on her command. Some nights, the ward became a forest, the air cool and crisp with the smell of pine. When she felt sentimental, the walls and floors shifted to a small village in central Turkey, before the soil had turned dry like chalk.

Most nights, she returned to Mecca. Even now, looking out at the palm trees framing the lake, still as statues, she forgot about the Exhibit.

Connor sat beside her. Dr. Hugh kept the fine lines around his face without the sadness of those last few days at the hospital.

He was not quite Connor, but he was enough. He told the same jokes, recalled the same stories, responded as Connor would. They even had the same fights – perfection would shatter the illusion.

Selma grabbed a beer. She turned to find Connor behind her, raising his own bottle in a toast. The drinks met, hers going directly through his hand.

"I feel like going to the sea today," she said. "That's the only thing about Mecca. There's a lake, but it's not the same – no waves, no breeze."

The Pacific stretched out before them. The smell of ocean water permeated the air, and she closed her eyes to the pleasant, rushing sound of the waves, the shivering of palm trees in the wind. North of their quiet beach, the lights of the highway trailed off into the distance.

"Do you ever think of leaving this place?" Selma asked.

"The ocean?" Connor asked.

"You know what I mean." But Selma's voice trailed away. She pushed aside thoughts of the Exhibit, of escape. It was the perfect beach, on a perfect night. Other nights would be less perfect, nights when she would despair and regret, plan escape or a final exit. For now, she was alive, and only the moment mattered. In that sense, it was real.

A Jaha in the Metaverse: a Short Story

By Fadi Zaghmout

Translated by Rana Asfour

Fadi Zaghmout is a Jordanian author and gender equality advocate. He holds a master's degree in creative writing and critical thinking from Sussex University in the United Kingdom. He has published five novels, including La Sposa di Amman *(MReditori, 2022) and* Paradiso in terra *(Future Fiction, 2023). His works have been translated into English, French and Italian. He is the recipient of the British Council's 2024 Study UK Social Action Award in the UAE.*

I don't like peculiar things, and I stay away from anything that's 'wild' or unconventional. I've become an expert at controlling every one of my body's movements. I adjust my muscles to position my body in a manner that conveys dignity and modesty, to self and place. And yet, for all my efforts, there's one muscle that always lets me down. A truant that singularly, stubbornly, opposes me. It insists on sabotaging every painstaking effort I make to present a wholesome, respectable image of myself. My failure to control it should not be consigned to a lack of trying.

And so, there's nothing I could have done any differently. I was betrayed at my most vulnerable, when all my defenses were down. The moment my eyes fell on the 'illustrious' Saeed, I knew I'd lost the battle. I blame HER. She went berserk, violently contracting, pulsating, and pushing against me like a caged madwoman. This time, we had both lost our minds.

I have a confession to make before I go on with telling this story. On that day, in all truthfulness and in fairness, Saeed

173

tricked us both. Concealed beneath his shells as some would say. Much like me, he too was in control of all his muscles, save one. But unlike my muscle, tucked out of sight and nestled deep within my ribcage, Saeed's rogue muscle occupied the entire space within his skull.

He confused me with his errant, crazy ideas. It left me constantly questioning whether I was even in love with him. And yet, as at the start of all relationships, the weirdness was entertaining. It made me laugh. He was funny, never insane. Honestly, I never thought he was being serious, or that any of his crazy notions would lead anywhere, and I never imagined, not in a million years, that I would become an accessory to their manifestation.

This takes me back to the first time we went out together. We had barely sat at a coffee shop in Abdoun, when across the street from us passed a strange-looking man, with disheveled hair and tattered, hole-ridden clothes. He seemed to be lost, confused, talking to himself in a way similar to those who've been struck in the mind. I initially dismissed him as a beggar, who, by force of habit, I always ignored and kept at a distance to avoid any trouble. Generally, that was what most people I knew did anyway. But not Saeed. He shouted out to the man to get his attention and beckoned him over with his index finger. As soon as the man approached us, pausing at Saeed's right, Saeed promptly initiated an extensive conversation with him. He asked him his name, inquired about his well-being, and his current pursuits in life. He didn't pause once to consider the man's unintelligible answers despite his obvious struggle to pronounce his words correctly. When Saeed had run out of steam, he pulled a dinar out of his pocket and placed it in the man's palm, then he asked him, "What do you think of my girlfriend?" When the man, clearly embarrassed, did not answer, he asked him, "Is she pretty?"

I was baffled and irked by Saeed's attitude. What man asks a male stranger to comment on his girl's appearance? Nevertheless, I held my temper in check, conjured a wane smile on my face, took a sip of my tea and placed it back on the table. Worried he'd try something else, I glared at him, and with my teeth clenched, I growled his name, as a warning.

Luckily, the embarrassing situation came to a quick conclusion when Saeed abruptly ceased his shenanigans. I chose to overlook the incident without making any comments. In a way, I was impressed by Saeed's self-confidence, the ease with which he communicated with strangers, and his magnanimous spirit that allowed him to break through class barriers. I convinced myself that Saeed possessed a superior ability to assess danger than I did. Consequently, I deemed his actions justified, as he had correctly discerned that the man had never posed the threat that I mistakenly believed he did. However, I did question my baseless anxieties, and my general prudishness. Wouldn't it be more beneficial if I were more spontaneous, and less reserved with others?

Indeed, that's what I set out to do. As I got used to having Saeed by my side, I also began to tentatively observe his every move. With a cautious admiration, I analyzed his approach, starting from the moment he involved himself in a situation, skillfully guiding his opponent towards a physical altercation, and then deftly diffusing the situation towards a peaceful resolution. He had this strange ability to turn the tables on his opponent and to end things in his favor. He had stamina for prolonged confrontations, seeming to enjoy the tense atmosphere they generated. He was my complete opposite. I, who unravels at the mere whiff of any impending calamity — whether significant or trivial. And yet, as the days passed, my attitude mellowed. I became better equipped to keep up with him on his adventures. In fact, I got so comfortable that when he started chatting with strangers out of the blue, I effortlessly joined in. I even invited them to sit with us so that both Saeed and I could get to know them. I started to accept Saeed's suggestions to go outside Amman and spend the day at the Dead Sea or take rides in his car to the outskirts of the city, even after the sun had long set. But I admit that my penchant for being spontaneous and adventurous was reserved only for the moments I spent with him. It is what made me feel connected to him and unwilling to be apart.

Saeed's adventures were many and his plans creative and unpredictable. However, he outdid himself on that day when he asked me to join him at one of the Sweifieh Village cafés. Taking advantage of my composed demeanor and harmonious disposition, he discussed what he perceived as a "groundbreaking and inventive approach" to our *Jaha*.[4]

"Hey, how about we have our Jaha ceremony in the Metaverse?" he blurted.

I laughed at what I assumed to be one of his whimsical jokes, even as he elaborated on how we would be establishing a precedent. My mood quickly sobered when I realized he wasn't sharing in my laughter.

"Are you serious?" I asked, slightly panicked.

"Absolutely," he answered me, deadpan, before launching into the rationale behind his crazy idea. "Tamara, my love, you know how difficult and narrow-minded your father is, and how mulishly obstinate my own is. It's going to be near impossible to join them under one roof because, if for any

---

4 "Jaha" is a traditional ceremony used to formally ask for a girl's hand in marriage. The chief/elder/guardian of one tribe/family approaches the chief/elder/guardian of another to request the hand of a girl in marriage. The women, including the bride, are not allowed to attend.

reason, they should disagree on something during the Jaha, they would instantly be at each other's throat."

He had a point. Our fathers nursed an old grudge that dated back to their childhood, when they shared the same classroom. The situation became tense again when a 'well-meaning' person took a photo of Saeed and me in his car and sent it to my father. He became extremely angry and contacted Saeed's father, threatening severe consequences if his son came near his daughter. His father had no choice but to submit to the threat. Out of respect for customs and traditions, he felt compelled, albeit reluctantly, to apologize for his son's behavior. He unleashed all his frustration on Saeed, promising severe punishment if his son did not sever all contact with me.

Neither of us complied. It wasn't a decision we could live with. I was deeply in love with Saeed and he never liked being told what to do. From our perspective, we had only two choices: either continue our relationship, with the risk of being exposed by 'well-meaning' people (of which there were plenty around) or try to convince both of our fathers that the best way to solve this problem was to publicly acknowledge and formalize our relationship through an expeditious engagement. The first option seemed risky because my father assigned my younger brother, who is a university student and a bit of a pip-squeak, to keep an eye on me. Even though I'd been able to outsmart him multiple times and appease him with a small payment and a mixed grill meal from Al-Quds restaurant, I couldn't completely secure his loyalty. The second option was just as difficult because it meant confronting, challenging, and pressuring our parents to support our relationship. Despite its obvious precariousness, we chose the latter. We figured that we were not only taking a well-thought-out risk, but also that our relationship would be shame-free and blessed by God. Even though everyone in my family supported my decision to marry Saeed, my father was hesitant to agree. However, I finally managed to convince him by threatening to elope with Saeed to another country.

I didn't disagree with Saeed's idea about a formal Jaha via the virtual world, even though the whole thing seemed a bit strange. I was certain that the meeting of our parents under one roof would, most likely, lead to unfortunate results. My pressing fear was that my father would reject the idea because he thought it would make our family look less important and devalue my prestige as a bride. But Saeed managed to convince him by promising that he would ensure various respected tribal leaders, influential people, and well-known personalities and 'influencers' would log into the event. Saeed also confidently assured me that it would be much easier for the elderly members of both families to attend the ceremony from the comfort of their homes instead of having to travel to it in person.

The following day, our minds firmly made up, we proceeded to the offices of a prominent Virtual Reality party organizer situated in the Abdali Boulevard area. We were fortunate to have secured an appointment at such short notice, thanks to Saeed's cousin who knew him. Otherwise, we would've had to wait for weeks, even months.

We were instructed to arrive, at least, two hours before the appointment to wait our turn in the crowded hall. We whiled the hours weighing out the various options on offer regarding the virtual halls, locations, and metaphysical spaces available in the Metaverse in order to arrange for reservations. I had to exert a doubled effort to curb back Saeed's enthusiasm to pick out the strangest locations. At a time when

I was looking for more elegant, and traditional options, Saeed was eyeing all that was different and wild.

He logged me into a hall that looked like it was on the surface of the moon, where alongside our guests, we would get to experience zero gravity. Saeed lunged into the air, laughing with childlike abandon, enjoying the lightweight feel of his body. "Ha! what do you think?" he said.

When he caught the look on my face, he quickly moved us on to another hall floating above a large expanse of red sand. A second later, when I realized we were on planet Mars, and before he could ask for my opinion, I forcefully leaned my body against him and pushed him out of the Metaverse. Regaining composure, I earnestly appealed to him to consider the matter more seriously. Subsequently, he opted for a spacious hall, suspended amidst the clouds, affording a panoramic view of the city of Amman. Despite the breathtaking view, the elevation made me nauseous. I grabbed on to his arm and begged him to take us back down to the ground. Although he immediately complied, it did not stop him from mercilessly teasing me. He continued to transition us between the peculiar and the wondrous until my mood completely deteriorated and I threatened to depart from the Metaverse, forsaking the project entirely. He nudged me to choose an ethereal hall located atop the Citadel Mountain, offering a splendid vista of the ancient city of Amman. However, by then, my patience had completely dissolved.

"We're looking for a hall to conduct our Jaha, a formal, might I add traditional, marriage proposal. We're not here for a wedding venue. Focus. What the hell is wrong with you?" I shouted, fuming.

Finally, it was our turn to meet Sami, the party organizer. As soon we told him what we were looking to do, he asked us to repeat our request to make sure he completely understood. "A Jaha? You want to organize a traditional Jaha in the Metaverse?" he asked excitedly.

When we, yet again, confirmed our request, he was ecstatic.

"Bravo," he said, clapping his hands in delight. "Firstly, I absolutely love the idea" he said, giving a thumbs up with his right hand as he began to list his reasons. "Secondly, I greatly admire boldness," he added, extending his index finger. "And lastly," he continued tapping his third finger, "I have a profound appreciation for our heritage, and I hold concerns about its gradual disappearance in the face of the challenges we face in preserving it in our modern era."

He expressed his support once again and surprised us even more by waiving his fees. He explained that he saw it as a small personal contribution to us as a couple, for our bold and innovative idea. His desire was to turn our virtual Jaha ceremony into a success story to show that the Jordanian identity could still be preserved even when using innovative methods that were more in tune with the current times. Nevertheless, my intuition suggested that he had seized upon a profitable venture. My suspicions were validated once he began to show us the different halls, categorized on price, guest capacity, and any additional bespoke amenities. Perusing the offers, I liked a hall designed by Zuhair Murad.

"It's very plain and expensive," Saeed objected. "Choose another one. It's wasteful to spend such a substantial amount on renting this hall for merely an hour."

At that particular moment, I desired no other hall. Moreover, I was absolutely not willing to give him the freedom to choose, especially after he had taken me on a dizzying, wasteful journey across the virtual universe, spanning from the Moon to Mars.

"Saeed, have you forgotten who the bride is here?" I said, compelled to remind him.

"You," he said

"Who will bear the costs of this ceremony?" I asked him.

"Your father."

"Okay. So, please back off," I said.

After successfully putting him in place, I carefully selected the necessary items and coordinated with Sami to arrange the chairs, tables, coffee cups, Kunafa plates and virtual sweets. These would be distributed to the guests after my father accepted the marriage proposal. I turned my attention to picking out a special design for the coffee cups that have become important at virtual celebrations lately. These cups are like beautiful works of art that people can keep and treasure as collectibles.

"Okay, how will your family members enter the hall?" inquired Sami, catching us off guard with his unexpected question.

I had assumed that the guests from my family would suddenly appear inside the hall upon logging into the virtual world, similar to the men from Saeed's family. Saeed seemed to be under the same impression. However, our assumption did not please Sami, who shook his head in distaste and stated, "This is disrespectful to you and your guests."

He suggested we allocate a nearby area for our guests to gather, where virtual luxury cars would be prepared to transport them to the hall. As this part concerned Saeed's family, I found him addressing it with enthusiasm, giving free rein to his ideas and asking Sami to add a group of camels and horses to accompany the impressive car procession.

"Camels and horses?" I said, surprised at his request. "Saeed, my love, have you lost your mind?" I asked.

He calmly turned towards me.

"Who is paying for this convoy?" he asked

"Your father."

"Okay, please back off," he said, a malicious smile curving his lips.

He had wasted no time in getting back at me for my previous comment. I chose to remain silent, refusing to engage with him. Instead, I ignored him and resumed my discussion with Sami in order to finalize the remaining financial obligations. We were offered the opportunity to enhance our documentation of the occasion by adding the services of a photographer who would take photos and videos from various angles, ensuring a comprehensive record of the event. We agreed. He graciously included special vouchers for the attendees, courtesy of Zara Metaverse Fashion store, offering discounts on men's suits and formal wear. The Jaha would take place in two weeks and so we left to notify our families.

On the day of the Jaha, my father, brother, and cousins entered the formal guest room and closed the door behind them to log into the Metaverse's hall for our Jaha ceremony. They had to be there before Saeed's family convoy arrived in the Metaverse. The women of the family congregated in the kitchen and living room at our house, because we had forgotten to add a virtual back room for them to gather in when we had organized matters with Sami. We asked him to include one a few days after we had seen him, but he told us that their company policy did not allow them to modify the spaces on offer. Unfortunately, our contract did not allow for the selected hall to be replaced with another. As a result, the women were excluded from the virtual event.

I now stood among them in the kitchen smiling, while attempting to conceal my nervousness from everyone.

Sometimes I looked at my watch and sometimes out the window, waiting for my cousin Kareem to show up.

"Where is Kareem, and why is he late?" I asked my uncle's wife, for the third time that afternoon.

"He's on his way, my love. He will arrive any minute. No need to worry."

But I was concerned, not only about his potential tardiness, but also about the possibility that he might break his promise to me.

Two days ago, I'd approached Kareem seeking his assistance in finding a resolution to my predicament. I had expressed my discontent regarding my exclusion from the Jaha ceremony. I desired to be present while the patriarch of his family formally sought my father's consent for my hand in marriage. When I voiced my wish to Saeed, he disregarded my request. It had meant nothing to him. He found my presence unnecessary and was ambivalent about helping me or even suggesting any of his ingenious solutions. So, following his usual madness, I decided to come up with a solution of my own. It was only natural for me to seek assistance from Kareem, renowned for his technical prowess in breaching cybersecurity gateways. He had promised to lend me his avatar to attend the Jaha ceremony.

Initially, he was taken aback by my proposition and promptly voiced his objection asserting that he had ceased engaging in any activities that violated the law. However, I was not taking no for an answer and knew exactly how I was going to make him concede. I remembered his infatuation with my closest friend whom I utilized as leverage. I proposed my help to set up a meeting with her in exchange for his assistance. He complied immediately and we mutually agreed not to tell anyone of our plan to avoid jeopardizing either party's safety.

I phoned Kareem several times but his phone was switched off which only made me more anxious and nervous. I almost called Saeed to ask him to cancel the entire thing, but I lacked the audacity to cause embarrassment to all parties involved. I couldn't stop looking out the kitchen window and fidgeted nervously, no longer caring if anyone noticed. When he finally showed up, half an hour later, I was ready to explode in his face. I pulled him by the collar and dragged him into my room closing the door behind us. I wanted to beat him to a pulp but I was running out of time. So, with frayed nerves, I watched him as he composedly pulled up a chair next to my bed and settled himself down.

I snatched his bag from his hands and retrieved his virtual goggles, hurriedly placing them over my eyes. "Wait, wait," he chuckled, amused, retrieving them back.

I looked at him, barely suppressing my anger and frustration, as he stood to remove a small device from his pants-pocket. He held it in front of my face and asked me to look at it so he could create an imprint of my eye. Once the device emitted a faint sound signaling that the scan was complete, he pressed tightly on the device releasing an electronic chip that he inserted into the goggles.

"All yours," he said.

I hurriedly placed the goggles back onto my eyes and logged into the ceremony hall looking around me to take in my surroundings.

I was happy to see the men of my family all dressed up and chatting as they awaited the arrival of Saeed's family. I looked around the hall and made sure that the arrangements we had agreed upon with Sami had been implemented as we had requested. There was a small table on which rested a pot of black coffee and the coffee cups with the designs I had chosen. When I picked up the pot, the pungent smell of ground coffee beans greeted my nose and I wished I could taste it. I was relieved to find that the photographer was also there.

A sudden jolt from behind caught me completely off guard. Uncertain whether it was one of the guests or Kareem, whom I had left in my room, I turned around to discover my pip-squeak brother smiling at me.

"Kareem!!" he greeted enthusiastically.

At first, I hesitated to give an answer for fear that my voice would give me away, but, steeling my nerves, I took the plunge nonetheless.

"Muhammad," I called with equal enthusiasm.

I was relieved when I heard Kareem's voice uttering my words. My apprehension completely dissolved, I spread my arms and hugged Muhammad and blessed him.

"Congratulations on Tamara's engagement. *Ogbalak*," I said. "Where is my uncle?" I asked, in an excuse to get away from him. When he pointed to where my father was sitting, I excused myself.

I made to head towards my father, but then changed course and rushed to the hall doors just in time to catch the resounding sound of approaching footsteps and the neighing of horses. I gathered that the procession bearing Saeed's family was about to arrive. I remained silent and watched them enter the hall. I was relieved to see Saeed enter the room with his usual stride, his flabby paunch and splayed knees; his avatar identical to his persona in the real world. I was suddenly seized by an irresistible impulse to run up to him and proudly reveal what I had done. I wanted to see his reaction when he realized that I had become as adventurous and daring as him. But I restrained myself and raised my hand to return his greeting after he looked at me and smiled, erroneously thinking that I was Kareem. After the men of his family took their seats in a row across from my family, I hurriedly looked around for a place to sit. When pip-squeak motioned to the empty seat beside him, I did not hesitate.

I surveyed the posse of men that Saeed had brought with him, and I smiled when I realized that he had kept his promise to bring along the finest. Present were three high-profile 'influencers.' One was famous for sharing captivating travel content experiences, another for mouthwatering recipes, and the third, who was the most well-known, for his hilarious sketches about married life and his daily pranks on his wife. At the end of each day the couple end up divorcing, only to make up again the next day and go through it all again.

The three sat sandwiched between Saeed, his father, and the senior members of his family in the front row. The prankster occupied the seat directly opposite my father. Judging by his seating position, I was worried that Saeed might have entrusted him with the task of giving the day's main speech to ask for my hand in marriage. Was Saeed out of his mind? I almost got up from my seat to scold him, but I quickly gave up the idea when I pictured the crowd's reaction at Kareem's unseemly and bizarre behavior. I closed my eyes and prayed I was wrong. Unfortunately, I wasn't. When I opened my eyes again, the prankster king had already risen to address the audience, evoking chuckles even before uttering a single word. It really felt like a stand-up comedy show than a formal gathering.

"Peace, brothers," he began. "Who among you is a married man?"

Hands were raised.

"May God help you. A necessary evil," he said, laughing.

The crowd broke out into peals of laughter, except for my father who kept a scowl on his face.

I was fuming.

Noticing my father's reaction, the speaker abruptly switched tactics, adopting a more somber tone.

"Joking aside, I would like to thank the honorable Naddwa family for choosing me to speak on their behalf on this day in which we seek the union of Tamara —our future daughter — to our son Saeed, according to the Book of Allah and the Sunna of his Prophet."

The speaker then turned to Saeed and motioned to him to take his place beside him.

"Brothers, our honorable groom needs no introduction nor anyone to vouch for him for he is a decent respectable and highly educated man, from an upstanding family." He abruptly broke off his speech, and turned, smiling, towards Saeed and whispered audibly. "Hey man, are you certain you don't want to change your mind?"

Saeed, smiling back, shook his head sideways, confirming his resolve to go through with this, while the men's laughter echoed around the room.

"Come again? You're certain? What sane person gets married these days?" he said, to the roaring cheers and heckles of the men in the room.

Just then, the influencer placed his hand on Saeed's shoulder and turned to address the crowd.

"It seems Saeed's mind is definitely made up. But before you agree to give him your daughter, I would like to ask him three questions. A simple test before you're stuck with him for life. Ready Saeed?"

"Ready," replied Saeed, nodding his head.

"Let's start with an easy one. If one day you should return home and Tamara hasn't cooked, what will you do?"

Before Saeed could open his mouth, the speaker had more to say.

"I'm going to give you three options to choose from: one: you divorce her, two: you send her back to her parents' house, and three: you order take-away."

"I order take-away," Saeed answered, oozing calm and confidence.

"Second question: If Tamara tells you 'My love, we must split the housework between us,' how would you react?"

"What? No options?" answered Saeed.

"Nope. You're on your own on this one."

"Tamara and I are agreed. We'll be sharing the housework between us. There's nothing wrong with that."

I did not like the questions or the manner in which they were being asked, but I admired Saeed's answers. Like me, it seemed that everyone was primed to hear the third question.

"Saeed, I think everyone agrees with me that you have successfully answered the first two questions. And now for the third and final question: Were Tamara and your mother with you on a sinking boat, which one of them would you save first, your mother or your wife?"

What a silly, redundant, and unimaginative question, I thought. But Saeed remained unfazed.

"You have to ask Tamara who she'll save first, because neither I nor my mother know how to swim."

I was bewildered at Saeed's candor and taken aback that he couldn't swim, the same man who bragged of his love for adventure and his fear of nothing. The same man who accused me constantly of being over-cautious and cowardly. I made a mental note to confront him about this later, even as I smiled and clapped my hands with the rest of the men.

"Our boy here doesn't swim," the influencer turned to address the row of men from my family. "Do you still want him? Or is this a deal breaker? I can assure you we still covet this union. Your Tamara for our Saeed. What do you say?"

Just then the speaker turned around and directly addressed my father.

"Hopefully, before the coffee gets cold?"

A deafening silence descended on the room as everyone held their breath awaiting my father's response. But it never came. My father remained as immobile as a statue. For a moment, I thought he was angered by the influencer's jester-like shenanigans and had made up his mind to block the proceedings. But, even then, he could've at least said something. The speaker addressed him again.

"What will it be, Abu Tamara?"

Again, there was no answer from my father.

Furious with my father's silent treatment, Saeed's father intervened. "Are you turning our offer down ya Abu Tamara?"

My father didn't so much as budge.

I panicked. What if my father took offense at Abu Saeed's tone, and things escalated into a fight. Thank God, I'd listened to Saeed after all and agreed to a virtual ceremony. I leaned forward in my seat to see if my father was angry or was merely collecting his thoughts when the loud-mouthed speaker's shouting intercepted my thoughts. "The man is not with us. Someone should check if he's alright."

Pip-squeak and I sprang from our chairs to check on our father. His avatar sat motionless. I was worried. Maybe he'd gotten angry and withdrawn from the ceremony before anyone could notice? But then, why would he leave his avatar behind? What if he'd had a heart attack or worse? Panicked, I retreated to the back of the hall and exited the virtual world.

"What's wrong? Did they out you?" Kareem asked worried.

"No," I huffed, running to the guest room in search of my father. The men were all there, including pip-squeak, their cyber goggles still on. I rushed to the kitchen to ask my mother if she'd seen my father.

"He's at the ceremony. What's happening? And where did you disappear to?"

There was no time to answer any of her questions. I needed to find my father. I looked everywhere but couldn't find him. That is until I tried the bathroom door and found it was locked.

"Baba?"

"Yes, my darling."

"What are you doing in there? They're all waiting for you at the ceremony." I couldn't believe he'd chosen the worst-timed moment to use the toilet.

"I'll only be a moment. I'm coming."

"Come on baba. Hurry up. The men are about to get up and leave. They have no idea where you are."

It took my father a full five minutes to exit the bathroom. The longest minutes of my entire life. As soon as he opened the door, I pounced on him and dragged him back to the ceremony as fast as I could. I sat beside him in the living room, not daring to leave him on his own. I didn't dare log back into the ceremony. I relaxed only after I heard him mutter a few words of apology, and then nod his head in agreement to something that was being said. He finally smiled, and offered his blessing.

It was finally over. The men had drunk the coffee and the women were busy, in the real world, distributing the kunafa in celebration. We had already made sure that the women in Saeed's family had received their order as well.

The following day, our unconventional ceremony made it into the local headlines, with a captivating title proclaiming, "A Father Answering Nature's Call Nearly Sabotages the First Jaha in the Metaverse." Our 'scandal' spread like wildfire as curious crowds scavenged the article for details.

No one found out about my role in the events of that day. It lingers as a memory that I still employ to shut down any outlandish ideas that Saeed suggests to me.

Today, several years into our journey together, Saeed is still busy racking his brain trying to find a solution for people seeking to relieve themselves within the confines of the Metaverse. He also insists that if we had not been the first to update the age-old Jaha, the ceremony would have altogether ceased to exist, bringing to an end a long-standing, and much-loved tradition.

Master of the Mediterranean

by Emad El-Din Aysha

Emad El-Din Aysha, an academic researcher, journalist, translator and author was born in the United Kingdom in 1974 to Arabic parents – a Palestinian father and Egyptian mother. He completed his PhD in International Studies in 2001 in the UK and has been living in Egypt ever since, working with such reputable institutions as the American University in Cairo and news outlets like The Egyptian Gazette *and* Mada Masr. *In 2015 he switched to writing science fiction and literary translation and studies and is now a member both of the Egyptian Society for Science Fiction and the Egyptian Writers' Union. He has translated a number of works and has two books to his name, an anthology (Arabic) and a non-fiction book he coauthored and co-edited* – Arab and Muslim Science Fiction: Critical Essays *(McFarland, 2022).*

> *"Love is the sea where intellect drowns."*
> *--- Rumi*

Tripoli by night is a wonderful sight... or so the song went. He had to see it for himself.

***

They let him in through the pinhole, like a native, of the giant gates of the legendary city. And it was a good thing too that he'd had to come in this inconvenient way.

Arab cities were always much more lively by night than by day.

A cool, fresh breeze flitted in from the coastline and to his amazement there was no smell of dust in the air. The weather was humid but not acrid. That made a refreshing difference, for sure. After his nostrils his eyes were greeted with something he hadn't seen except in black and white newsreels.

Old-fashioned billboards, painted by art students, decorated the skyline, and shone on by energy saving lights powered by solar cells *so* sensitive they could snatch the delicate moonlight out of the air and convert it into raw electricity. The students weren't paid, as such. They had money deducted from their tuition fees, and if they doubled in chemistry or physics they got a giant discount. Foreign exchange students from the lands of Da Vinci and van Meegeren were flocking to the shores and draining the talent pool up north. And the billboards themselves were painted in non-toxic paints laced with holographic granules, after all. The substance gave you a three dimensional image that chased you wherever you went, at whatever angel you chose to look at it from. No wonder the movie theatres were brimming with customers, with the internet finally meeting its match, the visitor thought. He'd read the report before coming here.

There were street hawkers but they weren't selling counterfeit goods or smuggled items. They were fully licensed and selling items for the co-ops of the war orphan funds. Everything from local handicrafts to roasted nuts to ladies handkerchiefs to iodine-reinforced balls of chewing gum issued by the ministry of health. They had their own union and made it a policy not to sell except domestically fabricated goods, and they had a dress code to boot. (All their flowing robes and baggy trousers and fez's were washed – in the Chinese launderer quarter – all ironed and spick and span. Their faces were as polished as their shoes. Their teeth were even shinier). They paid taxes like everybody else and had to abide by consumer protection laws with weekly, and sometimes daily, inspections. They even paid rent so as not to tread on somebody else's turf and cause a glut in the market and push prices down too far, both for them and the co-operatives. They all stood at evenly spaced intervals so as not to block people going back and forth in the crowded streets of the night-time city that never slept.

Oh, with one proviso. They weren't allowed to sell their wares in front of mosques and places of worship, among other centres of cultural life, such as theatres, hospitals, cinemas and agricultural libraries.

He passed by several sushi bars, all run and frequented by locals, with seaweed menus displayed proudly to onlookers. (The brand name, chefs, and the accounts were Japanese, however).

Looking at the fine print, on the chalkboard displays, he saw that the seaweed was harvested from the seaweed farms in the so-called territorial waters of the City, which stretched almost from one end of the Mediterranean to the other. Their formidable ships – even from the civilian cruiser he'd taken to get here – struck fear into the hearts of anyone who dared spot them from miles and miles away, and the immediate vicinity of one of their ships *counted* as territorial waters. A walking, talking island that could trawl the seabeds for anything it liked, and attach seaweed and corals and barnacles and pretty much everything to their habitat fishnets.

At this rate it wouldn't be long before they started exporting seaweed, to the Japanese. And the worst of it was the city had no shortage of veggies to consume, with the string of agricultural communes surrounding the walls of the city, which were in turn enclosed within a lower, wider set of walls.

They built everything from environmentally friendly

cars that were fed crude-oil substitute to building ships for Tripoli's merchant navies and their patrol boats and battleships which moonlight as tax collectors – protection money from anyone who dared to cross their path outside their territorial waters. No wonder he'd had to move in through concentric circles of fortifications just to get to the main gate. They weren't taking any chances here.

How much he regretted not taking a plane, but budgets were strapped as it was, even in his 'critical' line of business. He could have seen it all from above, images flowing up to draw you down to the light canopy below of the hustling bustling metropolis. Europe, whenever you slid over it at night, was the new *dark* continent. Factories didn't need people any more and could run day and night, so people were flocking away from the cities to the countryside, and the blasted trans-European agricultural complex was driving farmers off their land to flock to the cities. (Europe had its own brand of Okies, as the saying went). He'd seen actual Spy Sat shots of migrant flows, side-by-side, like oxygenated and unoxygenated blood cells clogging the same ventricle as they tried to move in opposite directions. It left you cross-eyed.

He shook his mind to clear it of the cobwebs that had accumulated in it. He decided he wasn't feeling like seafood tonight so he thought better of it. There was no shortage of mutton and poultry on display, along with the Mongolian bull meat restaurants, but he decided to leave food till later. He wanted to feast his eyes on enough of the city before having something like a plankton-stuffed cannelloni and some freshly squeezed Jaffa-orange juice to go with it or a... did he see that right? Ersatz mineral water? The plates the meals were served on were also made of ersatz porcelain. He'd have to inquire later.

Walking the streets, taking in the other inexplicable pleasantries, he found himself in front of an advert that he couldn't quite comprehend. It said, 'Haircuts for FREE'. Surely it meant something else. It said the same thing, three times over – in Arabic, English and Italian. The word 'free', was there, over and over again.

He decided to risk it. There was *no* shortage of barbershops, that was for sure.

***

It was a growth industry, and that was putting it mildly. Where he came from, you had whole streets that specialised in things like mobile phones or hi-fi systems. Here you had rows and rows of barbershops, working night and day with a distinct 'buzzing' hanging in the air.

The barber's like every other shop or café or restaurant, always had a row of potted plants on the outside, ranging from date palms and fig trees (squeezed into bonsai specifications) or good old-fashioned cactuses with prickly pears for the kiddies. He came in and his sharp eyes picked up someone busily sweeping away the hair off the ground into a set of giant paper shopping bags.

Sitting down, he was prepared to be disappointed. He felt like he was on a ranch, but he found some other foreigners there, and they were having fancy hairdos using good old-fashioned scissors and hairdryers. It was the natives who were being sheared like lambs.

Then he noticed a number of individuals, natives again, walking further indoors into what looked like a changing room, with further buzzing sounds, only for them to come out and hand over brown paper bags to the proprietor. They looked thoroughly refreshed.

What had they been doing there, he wondered, and by themselves? Some came out with the same shaggy curls on their heads as they'd gone in with.

Curiosity loosened his tongue and he asked. The boy

196

working away on his hair – it was straight so it gave the boy pause – answered while deciding on an appropriate strategy for tackling the man's foreign scalp. "They are cleaning zem selfes up!"

"I don't follow."

"Mr, do ze woman where you come fromed like ze hair in the pitts and ze bad smells?"

"Uh, no, they don't?"

"Chest hair is one sing," the boy said while beating his chest proudly. "But the pubis is something else entiredly," he said in his delightfully broken English.

It finally sank in. "That's rather disgusting, don't you think?"

"Hair is hair," the still too young man said while struggling with the gentle strands of the foreigner's hair. It stubbornly refused to stand up. He was still an apprentice.

"But, don't you at least set a charge for...," he gestured to the dressing room.

"We are all paid, and handsomely, by the state to provide this essential service," the proprietor finally spoke.

"What's so *essential* about it?" the visitor had to ask. He couldn't believe his ears.

"Do you think this is just for beautification, sir?" the man said at great length, stretching the words to breaking point.

"Well, yes, naturally," the visitor lied. There was so much lack of decorum in this place, he positively loved it. If it was anything he hated, like back home, it was etiquette and the spaghetti pool of rules you had to follow everywhere and everywhen.

"Well, you are wrong," the man said with a strangely acidic tone. "The hair, we hand over to the agricultural waqfs..."

"The who?" It sounded like a sneeze to his delicate eyes.

"Agricultural charities," the chief barber said reluctantly. "They are in charge of converting it to fertilizer, at no expense to the tax payer. It seems only fair, that we give something back for all that we take from the bounty of nature. And tax free."

Made sense, including the tax part, but for... fertilizer!

"But... you've got camel turds, don't you," the visitor asked.

"But of course, and cattle turds, and goat droppings. And ostrich droppings. But those are for export, and for bio-fuel." They had crap converters too, fortunately kept at a safe distance, outside the walls of the city, with rose gardens and jasmine and oleander to cover up the smell indoors, so to speak.

It beat the petroleum industry to a standstill, scaring off the evil oil companies that had divided the country up between them for so long in the first half of the 21st century. They converted a lot of that animal manure – and they had a *whole* lot of manure, from the camel caravans and goat herds that came to their doorsteps from as far off as South Africa to South Korea, every single day of the year – they converted it into crude oil. The trick, with oil, was the grades of the stuff, heavy, light, medium. They still had a smattering of crude in the desert sands, left from all the pilfering of the foreigner conglomerates, and it was all one lousy grade of crude, which put off customers. So they 'blended' the heavy, low quality stuff they had left in their oilfields with their lighter synthetic grades and put it on international oil tankers, on the condition that the tankers docking in their harbours be accompanied with a heavily armed frigate to make sure that they delivered on time and only to certain designated customers.

The visitor had read it all in myriad reports, but he had to see it with his own eyes to believe it. He couldn't wait till daytime when he could 'see' everything in the glory of the sun. He sighed and resigned himself to his fate, reclining further into the chair for the young boy to struggle with his too smooth European hair. Or yellow hair as they called it here.

Looking in the mirror in front of him as the boy hairdresser struggled away, the visitor almost noticed the proprietor staring at him, with his green eyes.

***

Ring, ring, ring, went the rotary phone in his room.

"Hallo, who is this?" the visitor asked with trepidation.

"So, hows' it going?"

"Who is this?" he repeated, more quietly.

"The line's clean, please don't fret," came the obtuse reply.

A sigh. "Fine thank you. I'm on holiday, *if* you remember." An image began to form in his head. A bow tie and a sardonic smile. And a waistline that began, or ended, at the skyline of the man's desk. That's how he preferred to look at him, from a safe distance.

"But of course," came the bombastic reply. If they'd been Americans, the man at the other end would have said, *Yeah, sure*. He would have also begun the conversation with *Hows' it hangin'*.

"To what do I owe this hon..."

"Is it as great as they all say it is?"

"In a manner of speaking," he said calmly. "I can certainly see the appeal."

"Are you joking? Malta's sided with them. The one island that stopped Hitler taking over the Mediterranean. How long before Sicily, Sardinia, Corsica and Crete follow suit, in alphabetical order. That's why you're there, isn't it?"

"That is *my* business, thank you. And you forgot Cyprus. Good night!" He shut the phone in the man's face.

He took causal peeks out the window and turned on the

TV to mask any noises.

Pacing back and forth like a caged lion, he finally sat himself down and found himself watching a late-night children's programme on goat-farming. Blankets made of goat-wool, it emerged, were so warm you could practically boil an egg in one. Medieval monks always wore goat-wool, that was for sure, and the Tripoli government had just signed a contract with the Jesuits and Franciscans to that effect. They were raising a whole new generation of Bedouins to be market traiders, under the guise of religious dialogue between the Abrahamic faiths.

More economics followed. Goats were sturdy as hell and didn't need imported animal feed, unlike dairy cows. The proportion of meat to gristle and bone and fat was favourable, compared to cattle. The sinews and inner intestinal lining of goats could be used for this, that and the other. The ratio of profits to initial investment cost was highly favourable, again compared to cattle. Then came the history lessons. Goats were used by the Arabs in Spain to turn arable land into pasture land, to maintain the readiness of the desert army. The Chinese never drank goat milk or any kind of milk because it reminded them of their savage, barbaric nomadic neighbours to the north, who also favoured pasture land. Europeans associated goats with Satan worship through their agricultural bias, but the joke was ultimately on them with what they'd done in the long run to their eco-system. A bunch of sheep herders as passive as the sheep they amorally shepherded. All the messengers of God in the Quran, Abraham and Moses and, and... were goat herders, tending their wayward flocks and, and...

He couldn't take it any more. His mind was overdosing on info. Better to call it a day.

***

Images flitted through his mind's eye as he tried to sleep. Walls crashing down around him wherever he went. A pair of eyes following him. The corridors of power.

The ground beneath his feet turned to sand. The stench of dust in the air. The horizon was black.

Papers strewn all around him. His whole life. Jotted down. Birth, life, death. Facts and figures. Assignments to nowhere.

He fished in his pocket and found a key. He used it on a door that emerged from behind him. Computer sounds as it unlocked itself. Passing through the threshold, he found a revolving door in the distance.

So this was it? Where his life had taken him. Where to from now? What good was he without a mission? A legacy?

A tune kept ringing through his head the whole time, haunting him like a dream within a dream. *Say, don't you remember, they called me Al; it was Al all the time. Say, don't you remember, I'm your pal? Buddy, can you spare a dime?*

***

He felt better in the morning. He'd got it all out of his system. That ghost from his past that was haunting him.

A new day, a new set of adventures.

He'd had a hearty breakfast of thyme and olive oil and wonderful Persian bread – so tasty you could eat it by yourself and consider it a meal – and some kind of milk paste that wasn't half bad. And several cupful's of sweet Moroccan green tea to wash it down, a multifaceted meal all served with Chinese porcelain. Homegrown, to be sure.

He'd been full up from the meal from last night, to be honest.

The pizza boy at the hotel – each one had its own delivery service – had misunderstood his instructions, and gave him a goat-meat and not goat-cheese special, and it was mountain goat too, so an aromatic delight.

Still, it did help him 'contribute' a little bit more to

this eco-friendly environ when it came time to offload his endeavours. It all went to the agricultural waqfs, and to think, economists where he came from were the ones fond of saying the more that goes in at one end of a donkey, the more comes out at...

Alas, it was his budding love for the city that helped him slip up, throwing him in the *slammer.*

***

"We don't take kindly to vagrancy," the white-faced judge assigned to his case said. He was sporting a fez with a legal insignia on it, speaking in English with a slight southern European accent. He was clean shaven and had a piercing gaze. He was also sipping coffee from an ersatz Chinese cup. (Have to lead by example, thought the visitor/slash defendant glumly, for a change).

"Vagr... I wasn't begging. I'm a tourist. All I did was...," the visitor protested.

"Putting money in the pockets of beggars is vagrancy enough in..."

"All I did was put a penny in the hand of..."

The judge didn't like being cut off but he forgave the foreign fool his eccentricities. "Those individuals you saw with their hands outstretched, if you'd bothered to ask, weren't begging."

"Then what were the..."

"They were checking for rain!"

"Oh," he said as flatly as he felt. It had never occurred to him, but the plastic canopies up and above gathered a lot of condensation and so little showers weren't uncommon from the mini-puff clouds operating within the many layers of the walls of the city. Solar-canopies made of fibre-optic threads powered the shops beneath them while maintaining the humidity level in the city streets to help the plant life flourish and keep the air clean of dust.

"It was an honest mistake," he added in protest. "So, what lies in store for me now? Work on your forced farms?"

The judge gave him a peculiar look, like he was talking to an imbecile, but he *was* a foreigner. Another sip of strong coffee and, "This is a first time offence, so you are free to go. It will not be tolerated a second time, do I make myself clear?"

"Certainly." The visitor stood up quickly, not eager to outstay his welcome, only to find the judge speaking to him as if he were in a lecture hall full of aghast law students.

"And for your information, the farms are fully voluntary," the judge went on. "That's the reason why they are so successful, beating your common agricultural policy, I will have you know."

"I'm well aware of how they are beating...," the visitor said, stopping dead in his tracks. He turned to face the judge, sitting himself down for the tirade he knew would come. He had a sip of ersatz mineral water, the only place you could get it free in this country. (The rock quarries here were rich in exotic minerals and with a little alchemy they could create imitation anything provided it had a couple of extra hydrogen molecules to differentiate it from the real thing. The Pharma companies did that in Switzerland and the US of A, so why not here for the common good? The mineral water bottle actually came with a brochure explaining it all, and the legal loopholes to boot).

"Communes do not work in your people's history, because they were either forced, at the point of a socialist gun, or manned by young intellectual enthusiasts who couldn't grow a spud if their life depended on it. And it didn't depend on it. They could always go back home to their parents and *suckle*." (The visitor blanched at the image, but he got the point). "And no geek of a boy is going to enjoy working with his hands, disaffected youth or no disaffected youth. *We...*," he said vaingloriously, "... we have 'refugee' labour of every kind and measure. Socialist farmers escaping your brand of forced capitalist-exploitation. Experienced middle-aged cultivators who want to live out the remainder of their days watching the land turn green, sniffing the sweet smell of roses and mint, and *nothing* more. Young start-up eco-farmers who don't know the phases of the moon but nonetheless are full of energy and ideas. All the while you, with your accursed robots are losing your most experienced factory workers too. The best labour money can buy, and we don't even need to buy it."

"Then what do you need walls for?" The pinhole door within a door he'd crept through when first coming here was a small door in a large gate, an old, old technique of insuring a city-state's security. The city gates were only ever open to visitors and merchants and peasants in the daytime. That's why a camel could never fit through a pinhole, as his own shepherd leader had taught them, something he'd forgotten until now. Conveniently. He slugged down more mineral water. He had a feeling he'd need it.

"To keep your kind *out*," the judge snapped back, politely. "Foreigners are more than welcome. They come to our shores, in boatloads, in exchange for our *protection*. But there is no telling how many foreign infiltrators populate their ranks. And truly, the walls of any city are its sons, adopted sons included."

"Protection? You live off *piracy*," the visitor threw back at him in this match of intellectual volleyball. The visitor knew what the judge meant by a city's sons being its walls. It was an old Spartan saying and this town was an oligarchy proving the myth of the Athenian democracy that Europe was.

"We're paying you back, after sucking our land dry of its

oil. For playing our people off against each other. Now the world is coming to our shores as Tripoli is the *blending* capital of the world!"

How true, the visitor thought. And from what he'd gathered talking to the inmates – all foreigners to a man – before the final pronunciation of the verdict, it wasn't just crude oil that they mixed and re-exported. It was also milk.

The people in charge of the city finances used the same logic to set up Tripoli's much vaunted milk blending centres too, using camel milk as a healthy if tasteless baseline for their exports, mixing it with goat milk for export to Arab countries, cow milk for Western clients, and soy milk for the Chinese. Camel milk was weak in lipids, which is why it never caught on for the cheese and yogurt industries, but it was full of vitamins and minerals, unlike traditional cow's milk. As a consequence, they didn't need to consume as many vegetables (seaweed helped too) to keep their bone density up. That in turn freed up more of the good greens for export from the communes.

"The thing that makes all the difference is... our hair," the judge said while stroking the minimal stubble on his chin. While the visitor didn't know this, the judge was making reference to an old Arabic saying ascribed to a Caliph who proudly declared that if there was nothing save a hair tying him to the people he would not break it. "It feeds the oil industry by lifting a burden off its shoulders and it feeds the milk industry by helping to grow the crops our flocks feed off. It is not just our barber shop customers who feed the industry, but even those who shave themselves clean early in the morning, before kissing their children before school, and shave themselves again late at night, before kissing their wives, in their own shaven spots."

No wonder permanently lasering your beards away was

disallowed here, the visitor thought as he scratched away on his bare scalp. As a foreign captive they'd shaved him *clean*, all the way down to his privates. So it had been that the nip and tuck he'd had the previous day that got him into trouble.

He'd got a tail put on him when the barber noticed he was asking too many questions. A barber who moonlighted as a judge. Nobody was allowed to have a desk job in this bastion of humane efficiency. That way he could afford to work for free in the daytime and save the taxpayer much needed pennies in a spot on the earth where the crime rate was virtually zero. The economic refugees who came here also worked part-time as the volunteer neighbourhood watch, and as informers

***

What a relief, he thought as he exited the courtroom, two young men who looked suspiciously familiar on either side of him. Maybe I'll send my kids to school here, he added silently to himself. They'd grow up to be tall and handsome and get steady jobs. The Tripolites controlled all the patents anyway. They had the best enforcement authority money could buy – their battle fleet of commercially converted vessels. Even their equivalent of the NSA was sea-bound half the time, snooping in on radio transmissions, checking for pirated songs and jingles.

Hell maybe his unemployed relatives could find work on the communes too. In the distant past the dregs of Europe had run away to pirate communes in Morocco, even in Herman Melville's day. Perhaps it was in his blood to do the same. He only had a short while before his European Union employers booted him out as it was. The whole reason he had come here. He thought he could extend his contract by impressing the bigwigs with his analysis of the Tripoli growth model.

The EU? What a gas. A bunch of bureaucrats working for

the private sector, bequeathing his generation, his parents' generation and his kids' generation a Dust Bowl all their own, coupled with Oklahomans. Homegrown to be sure. The man who'd pestered him in the middle of the night was a rival employee. Not his boss or case officer, economic intelligence notwithstanding. (Thank heavens the barber hadn't authorized a tap). He no doubt wanted to steal his report and get a promotion. It had come to this. A pencil pusher envying a glorified accountant.

Finally exiting the foreboding building he found the title of the place not to be the High Court of Non-Appeals or the Self-Righteous Penal Farm but the 'Tripoli Political Economy Club'. More commonly known in the West as the 'Anti-Adam Smith Institute', the *one* place in the world where central planning actually bore fruit. If only he could join them, an Adam Smither himself. But he still had his severance pay to consider.

Acknowledgements

Special thanks to my dearly departed friend Caryll Faraldi for information on voluntary socialist communes in Italy, which I used as a model for the story. (That quip about an egg boiling in a shawl or scarf I actually heard, but I think in reference to cashmere, and the donkey analogy is actually by economists). As for the barber shop idea, that was the whole inspiration for the story and I got it while actually having a haircut, seeing all that wasted hair being swept away for the garbage. Such an environmental waste!

Arabic SF – The Hope for a Better Future and Past

By Emad El-Din Aysha

To go forwards you have to go backwards first, or so they say. There certainly is great truth to this maxim when it comes to Arabic science fiction. To understand Arabic SF in its current state you have to put it in historical context, see what went on before and so how far (or little) we've come. To understand Arabic SF in general you also have to see how Arab authors, whatever their age, themselves go backwards in time to myths and epics and different eras in Arab and Islamic history, trying to stake their claim for the future by deciding on the meaning and significance of their past. The quest for an identity, in a word. But first on the tortuous origins and the multiple birthplaces of Arabic SF.

You can't separate the Arabs from their surroundings any more than you can disentangle Arabic SF from its cultural and political context. If anything we are more influenced by our non-Arab neighbours than we are influenced by each other as Arabs. As it's been said historically, Mosul is closer to Syria and Turkey than it is to the rest of Iraq, certainly in its trade. And so with science fiction. Muslims started writing SF in Turkey and Iran, and a slew of Lebanese and Syrian Christian writers embraced late Ottoman Utopianism, ironically looking forward to their countries' independence and the prospects of pan-Arabism. Hence these names, Francis Marsh (1836–1873), Adeeb Ishak (1856–1885), Farah Antione (1874–1922) and Michelle Al-Saqal (1824–1885). Egypt only caught the bug in the early 20th century with Musa Salama's novel *Introduction to an Egyptian Utopia* (1924), and even then a Lebanese author, in Egypt, was hot on his heels with Georgy Zidan's 1927 article "Prediction: Egypt and the World in the Year 2000", replete with open air villas and ancient Egyptian style decorations and furniture.

The only other example of early Arab SF was the (unfinished) Tunisian novel *The Lost Continent* by Sadek Rezgui (1874-1939), also looking forward to his country's independence. Note that the Levant and the Maghreb (Arab West) are the much more cosmopolitan and internationally connected parts of the Arab world, on account of expatriate communities or religious or language connections. The bulk of Arabs are in countries like Egypt, Iraq, Sudan, Libya and Saudi Arabia and they are much more cloistered and so less prone to taking up literary trends from elsewhere in depth. Egypt only really got on the SF line in the 1950s-60s thanks to the valiant efforts of Yousif Ezz Al-Din Issa (1914-1999) and Tawfik Al-Hakim (1898–1987) and then Mustafa Mahmoud (1921–2009), thanks to the Arab world being captivated by the Space Race. There was even a flurry of modernist poetry at the time talking about science and an industrial future. By the 1980s however that passion had fizzled out. Algeria and Morocco were a little bit luckier with early forays into SF in the 1960s-70s but again the key word is sustainability. Ironically Tunisia stopped writing SF after independence, seeing social realism as the true tool to advance the nation, a common trend across the Arab world. Not least in Egypt, the literary heartland of the Arabs on account of Naguib Mahfouz and Yusuf Idris and Taha Hussein and Ihsan Abdel Quddous, etc. For Egyptian readers, and the critics, SF was seen as a luxury for the rich and airy-fairy dreamers and no different than fantasy and surrealism. Even Mustafa Mahmoud and the literary giant Tawfik al-Hakim stopped writing SF almost as soon as they took it up.

Now to my initial thesis about the looking backwards of many futurist Arab authors. You always find traces of the past creeping in through the backdoor, if not explicitly incorporated into the world-building of the future text. You could see a hint of this already with Georgy Zidan's article and this streak of retro-modernism or Islamo-futurism, very prevalent in the current phase of Arab sci-fi. I translated Ahmed Salah Al-Mahdi's steampunk novel *Malaz: City of Ressurection* (2017), and in this post-apocalyptic Egypt you have two power centres, the city-state of Malaz in the north run by a warrior caste like the Mamluks, and Abydos in the south which has reverted to the ancient Egyptian gods and a priestly caste. They both have to revive the technologies of the past – a combination of gunpowder and energy cells – to fight a war for dominion. The upshot is that both cities are fully functional with clean streets and beautiful architecture; Medievalism is not being used in a bad away. If anything losing touch with the past is proper with the people of Malaz (or 'haven' in Arabic) because they are no longer Muslims, whereas the hero is named Qasim, in reference to the Prophet Muhammad, and modelled on the Mahdi-saviour in Islamic lore. Al-Mahdi is quite a progressive guy. Ammar Al-Masry, a very conservative Egyptian author, has explicit debates in his novels about East and West and the need to learn from each other to stop science getting out of hand. In his first big hit, his *Atlantis* trilogy, you have explanations for the story of the Flood and the legend of the lost civilization. This is an alien invasion epic with robots rebelling against Asimov's laws. I regularly incorporate past technologies and social mechanisms into my stories, including the one published here. In point of fact, of all of my stories, the one that Ahmed Al-Mahdi likes the most is "Demigods in Time", a time-travel story with Gilgamesh as a central character – the prototypical hero of legend. When Gilgamesh encounters an Arab boy from the future, his mission in life from then on is to use the past of lost or destroyed civilizations as a guide for the future. (Ahmed actually chose the title for me).

Dr. Hosam Elzembely, the founder and director of the Egyptian Society for Science Fiction (ESSF), has described the post-Arab Spring phase of Egyptian SF as the authentication phase where young aspiring authors have stopped imitating Western SF and are struggling to define their identity as Arabs and Muslims. Dr. Elzembely himself has a string of novels written at the turn of the century where you have Arab-Islamic Unions and Muslims becoming leaders of science or space explorers. His latest novel *The Last Voyage* (2023), has a handful of Egyptians trying to colonize Mars with Sufism playing a key plot point and theme. There's even a roboticist who programmes his own machines to break Asimov's three laws, quite deliberately bequeathing them a soul.

A Syrian researcher and author, Mohammed Abdullah Alyasin, has stumbled onto much the same set of conclusions looking at Arab and particularly Syrian SF, with authors from the 1970s onwards literally copying from novels and stories written in the US (or Soviet Union), just with names of the characters replaced with Arabic equivalents. Therefore, Arabs aren't building themselves in their future texts, they are *re*building themselves. Reviving their glory days, in a new fold. And it's not just Muslims. I was chatting once at a history event with a researcher about how inclusive the Islamic past once was, on account of Levantine Christians coming to Egypt in the 19th century. He replied this was the result of a shared Ottoman identity that allowed Arabs, whatever their faith, to open shop anywhere in the Arab world. The publishing industry in Egypt was begun by Syrian and Lebanese Christians including Georgy Zidan. One of his specializations as an author was historical novels dealing with epic heroes like Saladin or the Mamluks who defeated the Mongol hordes and saved Islam. A fellow Christian established *Al-Ahram* newspaper, which literally means The Pyramids (of Giza), glorying in Egyptian as well as Arab nationalism and pan-Islamism. Ottoman Utopianism itself was pan-Islamic, with modern institutions and technology incorporated into an Islamic fold. (Secular Turkey forgot all that and it took quite a while to get their sci-fi ball rolling again). Looking at the bookshelves and book stands, you do notice an increasing number of Christian names popping up on the covers of SFF works, at least in Egypt. Lebanon is already a Christian country and has names stretching from Canada to Australia. One such name, Jeremy Szal, makes references to djinn in his cyberpunk story "The dataSultan of Streets and Stars" and *The 1001 Nights* no less.

This puts us on parallel tracks with SF from the Global South, especially powerhouses of SFF like Afro-futurism. Alternative history is particularly indicative of this. Witness titles like *2103: The Return of the Elephant* (2005) by Tunisian author Abdelaziz Belkhodja, where the narrator is an American student in the resurrected city of ancient Carthage in a future world where Westerners illegally migrate to North African shores desperately in search of jobs. *If Hannibal Returned* (2005) by Al-Hadi Thabit focuses on what the Carthaginian hero Hannibal the Great would think of the modern world. Likewise you have the Saudi author Yasser Bahgat's novel *Yaqteenya: The Old World* (2015) where Muslim Spain isn't destroyed by the crusaders and as a consequence the civilizations of the native Americans aren't destroyed either, with Arabs discovering the new world. You get the same brave themes and historical constructions in Afro-futurist literature with classic novels like *Lion's Blood*

(2002) and *Zulu Heart* (2003) by Steven Barnes and polyglot empires like 'Bilalstan' populated by Zulus, Indians, Arabs and Aztecs. (Bilal is the name of the companion of the Prophet Muhammad, a convert who was originally an Ethiopian slave).

This backwards to go forwards march doesn't just apply to themes – history, religion, identity – but also to style, a subtle point most observers might not catch on to. Dr. Elzembely has pointed out, more than once, that he was enamoured by *The 1001 Nights* growing up and that his first childhood attempt at an SF novella was written in a fairytale mode. (He actually showed it to Mustafa Mahmoud, a family friend). Reading his 2001 novel *The Half-Humans*, a space saga, you found the heroes confronted repeatedly by 'riddles' while on the enemy's turf which is a classic technique from fantasy literature. The same goes for his latest novel *The Last Voyage* where you have seven characters each telling his tale over seven days is classic Shahrazade storytelling but is meant, at the same time, to serve the more modern purpose of using flashbacks to flesh out world-building and characterisation. Ammar, discussing an early draft of his Atlantis story, has heroes in a tower learning to use their new powers responsibly. I replied immediately that this sounded like *The Sorcerer's Apprentice* and he answered in the positive. He explained that he wanted to create a new blend of Arabic and foreign fairy-tales and splice that into his science fiction. When his novels finally came out you found talking, walking trees and character names out of Tolkien!

Ahmed Al-Mahdi was raised by his grandmother on epic tales, most Arab SF authors write fantasy and horror too, and I had a little fantasy drummed into me by my grandfather. An Iranian friend who has a cyberpunk novel set on Mars also used the literary tool of having a brother and sister separated in their early childhood only to be reunited in the future and he confirmed to me that this was a deliberate borrowing from *The 1001 Nights* and that he insisted on taking its literary guide. This is interesting and indicative in itself, but portends well for the global sci-fi canon, expanding on themes and subject matters and birthing new subgenres and expanding the reservoir of literary techniques at our disposal. In the case of Egypt there has been growing interest in ancient Egypt and many a novel cover with pyramids and other paraphernalia from that long gone world. Admittedly there's more of this revivalism in Egyptian horror and fantasy but you are getting new and original blends of genres in this current SF phase. One novel I've recently read, *Metaverse* (2022) by Mahmoud Fikri, has a curious blending of cyberpunk paranoia, time-dilation, genetic hybridization and religious themes. Here the gods depicted on the walls of ancient Egyptian monuments, half human and half animal, are actually genetic combinations relying on ancient alchemy while the virtual worlds of the metaverse are actually parallel dimensions containing in them your qarin [devil assigned to you by God, or evil twin soul]. He also has a dystopian future world where Egypt is shrouded in darkness because of a nuclear reactor explosion in Europe –a particle generator trying to break into the parallel worlds – and social media as a monitoring system using microprocessor implants to record your dreams. (Notice the symbolism too, of the West leaving us in the dark). I queried him on this point since he anticipated what is actually being pushed now, by Elon Musk, and he said he'd been following the news for a long time and took the next logical step in his novel. Metaverse itself is a sequel to a horror novel with no SF in it.

From dialoguing with horror/fantasy authors relying on ancient Egyptian motifs for their works, you find a growing confidence when it comes to ancient manuscripts or potions or hexes used to face up to Satanic plots involving foreign masonic-type organizations. I'm getting this from Asmaa Alyamani, an aspiring SF author herself. This is not completely unprecedented since Mustafa Mahmoud and also Nihad Sharif (1932-2011), the dean of Arabic science fiction, used numerous ancient Egyptian references. But again the question is *sustainability*. It's sustainable now and across numerous genres and genres that are cross-pollinating and giving birth to new subgenres; ones I can't even label.

So all in all the prospects are good and getting better. It's just up to the publishing industry and the critics to catch up in the meantime. Let's hope this collection of translated stories does the trick.

Author's Note:
The historical comparisons made here are primarily drawn from our ESSF book, which I co-authored and coedited with Dr. Elzembely, 'Arab and Muslim Science Fiction: Critical Essays' (2022).

Table of Contents

Made in United States
Cleveland, OH
14 April 2025

16100532R00127